Kate and Jolie

"Is there something I can help with downstairs?" Kate asked.

"Only if you're strong enough to throw people out of the house," Jolie said. "We've been trying to find maids ..." She stopped, embarrassed. "Household help, people to do the hard things . . ." She stopped again.

Kate's dark green eyes were unblinking. "It's all right to say 'maid,'" she said stiffly. "I know what I am."

Kate turned her back pointedly and smoothed the blanket under big, strong hands. Jolie saw her own reflection in the mirror over her father's dresser. Her cheeks were practically *purple*.

"I'll leave you to your work," she said haughtily, and as she walked out of her father's room, she thought—for a moment—that she heard Kate's smothered laugh.

Drat that girl. *Damn* that girl!

OTHER SPEAK BOOKS

A SEA
SO FAR

Jean Thesman

speak

An Imprint of Penguin Group (USA) Inc.

SPEAK

Published by Penguin Group

Penguin Group (USA) Inc.,

345 Hudson Street, New York, New York 10014, U.S.A.

Penguin Books Ltd, 80 Strand, London WC2R ORL England

Penguin Books Australia Ltd, 250 Camberwell Road,

Camberwell, Victoria 3124, Australia

Penguin Books Canada Ltd, 10 Alcorn Avenue,

Toronto, Ontario, Canada M4V 3B2

Penguin Books (N.Z.) Ltd, 182-190 Wairau Road,

Auckland 10, New Zealand

First published in the United States of America by Viking,
a division of Penguin Putnam Books for Young Readers, 2001
Published by Speak, an imprint of Penguin Group (USA) Inc., 2003

1 3 5 7 9 10 8 6 4 2

THE LIBRARY OF CONGRESS HAS CATALOGED THE VIKING EDITION AS FOLLOWS:

Thesman, Jean.

A sea so far / Jean Thesman.

p.   cm.

Summary: After surviving the 1906 San Francisco earthquake and fires,
two teenage girls, a wealthy semi-invalid and her hired companion, travel
together to Ireland and discover they share much in common, from a
love of romance novels to grief over the loss of their mothers.

[1. Sick—Fiction. 2. Social classes—Fiction. 3. Earthquakes—Fiction.
4. Orphans—Fiction. 5. San Francisco (Calif.)—Fiction. 6. Ireland—Fiction.
7. California—Fiction.]   I. Title.

PZ7.T3525   Se 2001   [Fic]—dc21   2001019592

ISBN 0-670-89278-5

Speak ISBN 0-14-230059-4

Printed in the United States of America

This is for my husband, in gratitude for his patient help with research—and his ability to find employment for Teddy outside the office.

Contents

Part One

The Earth Shook, the Sky Burned

April 18, 1906

CHAPTER 1

Kate

KATHERINE KEELY woke with a start shortly after midnight, certain she had heard her aunt call out. She held her breath and stared into the dark, forgetting for a moment that this was not the bedroom she had slept in for most of her fourteen years. But then, recognizing the feel of the bed, she let out her breath, exasperated. She had not slept all through a single night in the two weeks she and Aunt Grace had lived in the small house.

She had had a nightmare, too, probably because of her conversation with Aunt Grace the evening before. Mount Vesuvius had erupted in Italy, and Aunt had quoted friends who believed that the volcano was the sign of the end of the world, which a certain almanac had predicted for 1906. That was ridiculous, of course.

But Kate had dreamed of a volcano blowing fire into the sky, and now she lay awake and restless, certainly not worried about natural disasters, but uneasy because her life was precarious enough. Did every girl without parents wake up at night fretting about money? Would she soon find herself one of the many who had left high school in order to work and help support their families?

"Kate?" Aunt Grace called out in the dark.

"Coming!" Kate answered grimly. She would never get any sleep! She felt around on the floor for her shoes, then groped across the mouse hole of a room. Her outstretched fingers rammed painfully into the door, and she exclaimed under her breath.

"Kate?" Aunt Grace called, louder this time.

"Coming! What is it?" The gaslight in the hall had been turned down to a small bead, and Kate turned it back up as she passed. Aunt Grace's door stood open, and Kate could see the frail woman sitting up in bed, clutching the sheet to her chest.

"I had such a terrible dream!" Aunt Grace exclaimed.

"About the volcano?" Kate sat on the bed and smoothed her aunt's hair. As exasperated as she felt sometimes, she wanted to protect this middle-aged relative who tried so hard to be a complete family to her.

Aunt Grace lay back with a sigh. "I was dreaming about your father, Kate. Here we are in this dreadful house . . ." She paused to sigh again. "And it's South of Market Street, too," she went on with a disdainful sniff. "As if any daughter of Thomas Keely should live in such a neighborhood."

"You like being next door to the Flannerys," Kate supplied firmly. "Go back to sleep and dream about the picnic we'll be having Sunday afternoon with them. Golden Gate Park, Auntie! You'll love it." She tucked her in as if her aunt were a small child and started back to her own room.

"Don't close my door!" Aunt Grace called out.

"I'm leaving it open," Kate said. "Mine, too. Call if you need me."

She would never get back to sleep now, she thought as she returned to bed. They had stayed up too late, drinking tea on the porch steps, watching the yelling, scrapping, carousing children in their neighborhood while darkness drew close around them and hid the shabbiness. Mrs. Flannery and her daughter, Ellen, had strolled over to join them, and they had listened to Aunt Grace's news of the volcano on the other side of the world.

Kate sighed and got out of bed again. Sometimes, when she was lonely, she would take her parents' photographs off the bureau and put them under her pillow. That night she also picked up the small green carved bead her mother had given her, wrapped it in an embroidered handkerchief, and slipped it under her pillow, too. Once more she lay down, wishing the night was over. Her last thought before suddenly sleeping was something her mother had told her about Ireland. "The green fields unfold and unfold and unfold before you," she had said. "Green upon green, right to the cliffs and the far sea beyond." The fields around San Francisco were brown most of the year, and no one described them as "unfolding." Kate slept.

She knew it was five o'clock when she woke because she heard the horse and wagon belonging to Tim Ross, the brother-in-law of Mary Flannery. He always came at the same time each day, and the racket from the horse's hooves on the street would wake Kate half an hour before Aunt Grace's alarm clock rang. Hugh Flannery had left school and worked in Ross's grocery story. He and his uncle went to the produce district every morning to pick up the fruit and vegetables needed for the day.

The horse's hooves clattered nervously, and Kate heard Hugh's uncle say "Tilly!" sharply. Still the hooves clacked and clattered, and suddenly Tilly screamed once, twice. Kate flew out of bed and snapped up the shade. Below in the street, Mr. Ross struggled to control the brown horse, but she reared and screamed again. Harness and shafts clashed. Ross swore as the horse and wagon carried him off down the street with him bouncing on the hard wooden seat.

Kate stayed at the window, wondering if the man would return for Hugh. The sun was not up yet, and an almost invisible crescent moon hung in the pale green sky. But there was no fog, and that was a blessing. The first birds should be chirping in the crooked tree next door, but, strangely, they were silent that morning.

Hugh, dark and lanky, ran out of the Flannery house, buttoning his brown jacket while he looked up the street where his uncle and the horse had disappeared. Kate saw him glance in the other direction and shrug.

"Is he gone already, Hugh?" she heard Mrs. Flannery call.

"Gone in the wrong direction," Hugh answered.

"Sakes," Mrs. Flannery exclaimed disgustedly. "What's got into that horse?" Their door slammed.

Kate went back to bed, although she knew she would not sleep. She should go down to the kitchen and build up the fire for breakfast, then check her homework one last time. When she first heard a distant rumbling, she sat up on one elbow, alert and curious. The pencils in the small glass vase on her desk tinkled musically. The floor shuddered, delicately at first and then it rocked and heaved madly while the rumble changed to a roar. The room tilted. *What is wrong?*

The house shook violently now as the roar turned to thunder. *Earthquake!* The bedroom twisted while dust and chunks of plaster fell in a torrent. The windowpanes shattered and glass sprayed across the room. The bellowing thunder went on, louder now. The light from one window was cut off abruptly, and horrified, Kate saw bricks from the chimney cascade past.

She was thrown from the bed to the floor, landing painfully on her side. The air was filled with dust and bits of plaster, and she could barely see.

On and on, the shattering roar continued, and the house shook as if an animal had grasped it and was killing it. Somewhere, something was torn apart with the shriek of twisted metal.

And then the roar died away. Silence. There was not even an echo. No one called or screamed or cried. The world had stopped and Kate was afraid to breathe. She was not sure she was truly still alive.

At last Aunt Grace called weakly from her room. "Katie, are you all right?"

"Yes," Kate said, and her voice shook. She got to her feet, crouching under the partly fallen ceiling and reached for her shoes, but the beast grabbed the house again, more raging and murderous than before. She fell sideways onto the bed, still clutching her shoes. We're going to die this time, she thought. It's going to kill us.

More of the ceiling collapsed, the floor buckled, and one wall fell away completely. For an endless time, she clutched the bed while it flew back and forth again and again. Then the shaking eased, the roar died away to a distant grinding rumble, and the quake finally stopped.

There was another silence, this time so profound that it seemed to swallow up the world. Kate took a shallow breath, waited, and finally pulled on her shoes, expecting the roof to fall the rest of the way and crush her. "Are you all right, Aunt?" she called out, afraid that there might be no answer, that she would be completely alone now, left to face the unimaginable.

"I'm all right," Aunt Grace answered feebly.

"We've got to get out of here," Kate said. "It might start again." As she got to her feet, she realized that she was holding her mother's photograph in one hand. She tucked it in her nightgown pocket and looked around for her father's photograph and the bead. Half her bed was covered with slabs of plaster. She would have to find them later, when someone could help her search. She climbed over the rubble on the floor and discovered that her door was jammed shut. She had to get out! There could be another earthquake any moment! She tugged at the door again, panicked now, and wedged her shoulder into the narrow opening but still could not get into the hall.

A strange dusty light shone into the room from the place where the wall had been, and for a half-mad moment she wondered if she should climb over the shattered boards and jump out of the house there. Her bureau was gone, along with the wall and the hooks that had held her clothes. There was not a sound outside, no voices, no screams, and for a moment she thought that only their house was damaged and no one knew what had happened to them. But then, in the distance, she heard the crash of something falling.

Terrified, she grabbed the edge of the door and pulled with all her strength, and finally made an opening wide enough to squeeze through. "Aunt!" she shouted. "We have to get out!"

The upstairs hall was littered with plaster, but her aunt's room was not badly damaged. She was struggling into a dress, and when she saw Kate, still in her nightgown she said, "You can't leave the house like that, Kate."

Kate, stifling an urge to shout, said, "I have no clothes. Most of my bedroom fell into the Flannerys' yard."

"I'll get you something of mine," Aunt Grace said briskly, turning to her bureau. Kate saw then that her feet were bare.

"Put something on your feet," she cried. "There's broken glass on the floor."

But Aunt Grace had yanked open a drawer and

tossed bloomers and a petticoat to her. "Here, child, and here's a chemise and stays, and you can wear my blue dress . . ."

Kate grabbed the clothes and ordered her aunt to put on her shoes. "And hurry!"

Aunt Grace obeyed, sitting cautiously on the edge of her tilted bed while Kate pulled the too-short linen dress on over her nightgown. She would worry about petticoats and corsets in another lifetime! she thought, both furious and frightened.

An ominous creak overhead startled Kate. She did not wait for Aunt Grace to finish lacing up her boots but dragged her out the door to the landing. "Wait!" Aunt Grace shrieked. "My pocketbook! We might need change for the streetcars."

She jerked loose from Kate and darted back into her room. With the bad luck of the Keelys, Kate thought, we'll have another earthquake while she fusses with her pocketbook. Change for the streetcars! Had she forgotten? We have no home except this one, no family left, and few friends well off enough to take us in. Where can we go?

"Here we are," Aunt Grace said as she stepped over the wreckage in the hall. "Dearie, smooth your hair. You look like a banshee." She plucked a bit of plaster from Kate's loose red braid and flicked it away.

Kate led her down the stairs that were littered with plaster and loops of wallpaper. The air was still thick with dust and soot. Kate could even taste it. She took only a brief look into the parlor as she passed. One wall was gone and half the room was filled with loose boards and shingles. Kate stepped out on the sagging porch and saw a new world.

The house across the street had collapsed into a mountain of boards, and a cloud of dust sifted over it. Several men stood nearby, silent, unmoving, apparently in shock.

All the Flannerys were outside, looking about them like stunned rabbits. Dark-haired Ellen, sixteen, kept one arm close around her mother's neck. The gray dust drifted down everywhere. On both sides of the street, houses had heaved sideways or lurched backward, sometimes with walls fallen away, and inside the bedrooms the beds and bureaus still sat upright, so that they looked like dollhouses. Every chimney was down. All the telephone poles had fallen, and Kate saw angry sparks in a heap of tangled wires. Part of the street in the next block sat two feet higher than before, and water from a broken main gushed out beneath it, creating a clean path in the rubble.

A line of half-clad neighbors, covered with grime, stood frozen in front of their houses. Everyone was silent, even the smallest children, as they looked at the wreckage. There never had been anything attractive about the block, but the Flannerys had lived there for years, and Mrs. Flannery had assured Kate and her aunt that there were worse places in the eastern part of the United States, and worse yet in Dublin.

Now four of the houses had been destroyed by the earthquake, and all of the others were damaged. But what amazed Kate most was the corner boardinghouse, which now was only one story high. It took a moment before she realized that it had collapsed into its basement, and now just the top floor sat above the street with muddy water bubbling out from under it. A man clad in baggy long gray underwear was helping another man out of what had been a third-floor window.

No one spoke yet. The silence was unreal—and wrong. People should be shouting or screaming after what had happened.

Without warning, the earth rocked again, roaring and twisting, and sending people rushing toward the middle of the street, away from falling bricks and boards. Kate saw a roof slide to a side yard while two pigeons soared away. A fountain of water gushed from a split in the street, and then it turned into a trickle.

The Costas' small terrier suddenly appeared from the wreckage of their house across the street, bloody, yelping shrilly, and snapping at the air. When Hugh moved to help him, Mrs. Flannery yanked him back, murmuring urgently, "You can't help. God bless the innocents."

Where are the people from that house? Kate wondered. She stepped into the street, but Mrs. Flannery pulled her back, too, and Aunt Grace cried, "No!"

Everyone nearby began moving then, as if released by Aunt Grace's cry. Some turned toward their wrecked porches; others embraced. Men gathered at the silent, collapsed houses and pulled uselessly at fallen boards. One called out, "Is anyone in there?" but no one answered him.

Mrs. Flannery's gentle plump fingers moved through Ellen's hair. "Ah, now, there's just a small cut on your scalp. Hoist up yer skirt, girl, and let's look at those bloody knees, too. Joe Flannery! I'll smack you flat for looking, you devil!" She aimed a slap at her eleven-year-old son, who ducked expertly and dodged behind Ellen, who grimly delivered the slap on her mother's behalf.

Across the street, the dog twitched on the sidewalk, whimpered weakly, and then, at last, curled still and silent.

"Don't cry, Kate," Mrs. Flannery said. "It's only the beginning. The Costas are in there, somewhere." She looked down at the watch pinned to her generous bosom. "Can you believe it's not yet a quarter to six?" She crossed herself and shook her head.

Gradually the neighbors began to salvage what they could, and they came out of their houses again fully dressed, sometimes even wearing layers of clothing, and pulling trunks and suitcases. Several men still struggled with the wreckage of the Costas' house, working silently and grimly. Down the block, a dozen men dug into the boardinghouse ruins. Water still bubbled from the wreckage but the stream was smaller now. Gas hissed from broken pipes everywhere.

Seeing other people retrieving things from their wrecked houses gave Kate courage, so in spite of Aunt Grace's protests, she dragged the wicker trunk downstairs from Aunt's bedroom. It held only a few clothes, a box of precious family photographs, and a spare blanket. The ceiling in her bedroom had collapsed completely, so she could take nothing from there. Later, she would wonder that she had not remembered to pick up a comb and soap from the bathroom or even a scrap of food from the damaged kitchen. The earth rumbled and shook again, and she hurried out to the street.

"This isn't much," she said. "Should we try to get out some of the furniture? Look over there at those people. They're trying to get their piano out the door."

"Someone will come along," Aunt Grace said absentmindedly as she watched a woman up the street carrying a cage with a shrieking white parrot out of her ruined house. A fat brown dog waddled behind, panting. "Don't worry, Kate. The police or somebody will be here soon and tell us what to do about everything."

Mrs. Flannery, tying a bundle of children's clothes on Joe's red wagon, glanced up and said, "I doubt we should wait. Look!"

Kate turned to see. A few blocks away, somewhere around Sixth and Folsom, smoke billowed up, and even while they watched, it turned from gray to black, and then she saw the flames licking underneath. In the distance, fire engines clanged.

"Look there!" Ellen Flannery said, pointing in another direction. "I see two—no, three fires. No, there's even more, Ma! The fires are everywhere!"

Deep inside the collapsed boardinghouse, someone began to shout, "Help us! Help us! We're drowning down here!" The men working there shouted conflicting instructions at one another and tore at the ruins.

Nearby, an old man with a blanket over his shoulders said, "They won't get them out in time." A rosary clicked in his fingers. "But it's better to drown than burn, and the fires are coming."

Kate exchanged a glance with Mrs. Flannery. "Let's

walk over to Market Street and see what's going on there," the woman said in a firm voice.

"Somebody's surely going to come along and help us," Aunt Grace said.

Almost ready to scream, Kate met Mrs. Flannery's gaze again. *No one was coming to help them.* There must be injured—dying!—people everywhere. Mrs. Flannery's eyes told her she was right. "We'll move along with the Flannerys, Aunt," she said, louder than she had meant to. "We can come back later to get out things."

With the help of Joe Flannery, they dragged their trunk along the street, avoiding the scattered debris. Mrs. Flannery, Hugh, and Ellen maneuvered the wagon, a suitcase balanced on an old baby carriage heaped with blankets and all of it topped with a sack of bread, and a well-wrapped oil portrait of the late Mr. Flannery.

"We can't leave the mister behind, God rest him," Mrs. Flannery said. "He always did say this town would fall flat one day. Joe, are you letting their trunk drag on the ground? I'll give you such a smack when I get hold of you!"

They knew the fire was catching up to them because they could hear it and smell the smoke. Everyone agreed that they should walk toward Market Street, where they would be safer. Kate wondered if they might need change for a streetcar after all—perhaps she and her aunt could find help in their old neighborhood on Russian Hill.

A team of sweating fire horses and a clanging pump wagon rushed past, clattering over fallen bricks and masonry. The old man with the rosary walking behind Kate said, "The water main's busted. Won't do them fellers in the boardinghouse no good."

Smoke rolled over them, and sparks and hot ashes showered from the sky. Joe Flannery cried out suddenly, clutching his singed hair. Mrs. Flannery tied her apron over his head like a kerchief. "No stragglers now," she said briskly. "Everybody, keep up."

"Someone's bound to come along and help," Aunt Grace said. No one responded.

When they reached the corner, they saw a crowd of silent people in the streets, moving north toward Market Street in a great mass. They were dragging trunks and loaded wagons, pushing tables on casters stacked with belongings, carrying bags and suitcases. An automobile honked its way between them, filled with grim-faced men. A crushed wagon and a gasping, dying horse half covered by bricks blocked part of the street. Was it Tilly? Kate choked on a sob.

The fire behind them was noisily consuming everything, crackling, hissing, humming. In the distance, someone screamed terribly, over and over. "The fire, the fire! Don't let me burn! Kill me now, *now*, don't let me burn!"

Suddenly they heard a shot, and the agonized voice was mercifully silent.

Mrs. Flannery crossed herself and began praying aloud. "Hail Mary, full of grace . . ."

CHAPTER 2

Jolie

JOLIE LOGAN, nearly sixteen, had promised her parents that she would not wait up for them, because they were going to supper with the Prescotts at the Palace Hotel after the opera and they would be late. But she had had no intention of keeping the promise and stayed awake reading *Green Mansions.* When she heard Dr. Logan's automobile stop beside the house, she hurried out to the upper hall, eager for one more look at the beautiful Worth gown Aunt Elizabeth had sent her mother.

Jolie still had not recovered from her battle with scarlet fever at Christmas, and she reached out to steady herself with one thin hand on the banister. The Logans came into the entrance hall below, Father tall and bearded, Mother slender and erect. Mrs. Logan's maid helped her out of her stiff brocade coat, and there was the wonderful dress, as delicate as gray fog and shimmering with crystals. Jolie saw her mother look up, as if expecting her to be there. "Darling, what are you doing out of bed?"

Mrs. Logan had smooth brown hair and bright blue eyes, and she was beautiful. Jolie had lost her hair during her illness, and now it was growing back, barely two inches long, pale blond like a baby's, and always concealed by a cap.

"I only wanted a quick look at you," she called down. She did not want her parents to see that she was having difficulty breathing again, so she did her best to grin at them and then backed away from the banister. Tomorrow she would ask her mother if she could try on the dress herself. A Worth dress! Aunt Elizabeth led an exciting life of travel, and she bought all her clothes in Paris.

The clock in the upstairs hall bonged solemnly. One o'clock in the morning. She had missed her chance to see Caruso sing in *Carmen*, and he might never come to San Francisco again. She had missed so much—everything!—in these past months.

She was back in bed with her glasses off and the sheet pulled up under her chin when her parents looked in the door. "Feeling all right?" Dr. Logan asked.

"I'm fine," Jolie said. Heaven forbid that he come in to listen to her heart again.

Her father nodded and moved away, but Mother lingered in the doorway. "Are you really ready to sleep? Perhaps I'd better get you a cup of warm milk."

"No, I'd rather hear about the opera," Jolie said. She

longed to ask if David Fairfield had been there, escorting his mother and sister.

"We'll talk in the morning," Mother said, smiling. She turned off the light and closed Jolie's door halfway, so that the hall light could shine in a little. Jolie heard the maid ask Mother if Mrs. Rutherford had seen her dress and the diamond earrings Father had given her for their anniversary. Mother's answer was lost when her door shut.

Jolie waited until the house was quiet, and then she got up again and turned on her light. Since her illness, she had hated the dark, but Father thought that she would be tempted to read instead of rest if she had a light. She read every night.

She fell asleep over her book, with her glasses sliding down her nose, but woke again much later, gasping for air. Oh, not again! She sat on the edge of her bed, coughing and trying to calm herself, but these terrible moments always panicked her. Relax and inhale slowly, she told herself. Never mine that your heart is pounding. This will pass. It always passes.

As the hall clock struck five, Mother hurried in, fastening her white silk dressing gown. "Trouble again, darling? I heard you coughing. Do you want me to get Father?"

Jolie shook her head, unable to speak.

"Would you like a cup of good hot tea?"

Jolie nodded. Hot tea often helped her.

Mother had been gone only a few minutes when the room suddenly jerked sideways and then back again. *What?*

The world around her filled with rolling thunder. The mirror over her dressing table flew off the wall and splintered on the floor. Then, while she dug her fingertips into her mattress to hang on, the room rocked violently. Books cascaded out of her bookcase, one shelf at a time.

Gradually the rocking stopped. Jolie sat very still. It was an earthquake, of course. They had had them before, but never such a sharp one. She saw broken glass glittering on the carpet. Her bedside table had tipped over, spilling her water tumbler. Her wardrobe doors had fallen open, her clothes in a jumble inside.

It began again, worse now. Something heavy hit the roof. The light went out, and the windows were nothing more than pale shapes in the dark room. Somewhere, more glass shattered. *Mother*, she thought, panicked. Where is she?

Then the rumbling and shaking stopped. Jolie waited to hear someone call out, but in the silence that followed, she only heard timbers groaning under the roof. The air was full of dust and difficult to breathe.

"Jolie!" Father cried suddenly from the doorway. "Are you all right?"

"Yes," she said, sitting up and moving to the edge of the bed. She could barely see her father across the room. "Is Mother all right?"

"Isn't she with *you?*" Papa exclaimed. She heard his feet crunch on broken glass. "Amy? Amy, are you here?" he called.

"She went down to the kitchen to fix tea for me," Jolie said, suddenly even more terrified.

"Get up," Father said. "Hurry." He pushed the draperies back from the broken windows, and she could see him then, dimly, in a room filled with dust. He grabbed her dressing gown from a chair and shoved shoes on her feet, then pulled her into the hall. The stairs had sagged away from the wall, but he led her down them quickly.

Mrs. Conner, the housekeeper, was already in the hall, her dark blue robe firmly tied around her stout waist and her gray hair twisted up into its usual bun. She followed them out to the porch, where Dr. Logan told her to find a place for Jolie to sit down. "But stay away from the house," he said. He ran back inside, shouting his wife's name.

"Did you see Mother in the kitchen?" Jolie asked Mrs. Conner. She pushed away the housekeeper's hands. "Did you see her?"

"I came straight through the hall," Mrs. Conner said. "But Joseph went to the kitchen to check on the stove. He'll take care of her."

The cook was with Mother? "Why don't they come out?" Jolie cried.

"I don't know. We must get to the street! No, don't look back!"

But Jolie looked behind her anyway. The chimneys had collapsed and Father's automobile was buried under bricks at the side of the house. Where was Mother?

"Why doesn't Father bring Mother out?" Jolie demanded.

But Mrs. Conner was propelling her firmly toward the house across the buckled street, where the Verts had assembled in various stages of dress. Mrs. Vert and Mrs. Conner exchanged whispers worriedly before they sat Jolie on a broken chunk of stone cornice that had fallen conveniently at the edge of a flowerbed.

"Now you stay here and don't move," Mrs. Conner said before she ran back across the street and into the house.

Jolie would have stood again, but Mrs. Vert pushed her down firmly and called her twelve-year-old daughter, Jane, to keep her company. Jane, her own wire-rimmed glasses crooked on her freckled nose, grasped Jolie's hand. "You're to keep very still and not get sick again," she said officiously.

Jolie stared at her. "My mother's still in the house," she said. Her terror was increasing. Her heart thudded in her throat and she struggled to breathe.

"Papa is bringing out a mattress for you," Jane said as she slipped one arm around Jolie's shoulders. "You mustn't talk now. Everybody's fine and we're to look at this as a great adventure, Papa says."

"Oh, here now, missy," Mr. Vert protested from behind Jolie, and he caught her as she fell sideways. She thought for a moment she saw her mother standing over her in the gray Worth dress, but she was mistaken. It was only the gray dust that fell everywhere, on everything, and the voice she heard was only Mrs. Vert's, calling her "Sweetheart."

Jolie heard voices and opened her eyes abruptly, terrified. But it was Mrs. Vert hovering over her. "Back with us, Jolie?"

Mrs. Vert and Jane made Jolie a comfortable bed at the edge of the street. Propped on pillows and struggling to breathe, Jolie watched Mrs. Vert pour a powder from a twist of paper into a cup of water. "Mrs. Conner says your father wants you to have this," she said as Jolie made a face. "He's taking your mama to the hospital in the Nickersons' auto now, and everything will be fine and you're not to worry." She tried to take Jolie's glasses but Jolie held them in place. She was nearsighted, and this was not a day that she would be content to see the world as nothing more than a blur.

"Is Mother hurt?" Jolie as Mrs. Vert held the cup to her mouth. "Is it very bad?"

"Your father says he wants to have her checked over at the hospital, that's all," Mrs. Vert said. "But he ordered you not to worry, and you know that girls can always trust their fathers. Now gulp this down quickly so you don't mind the taste."

Jolie obeyed. Jane, who had been hovering beside Jolie, settled Jolie's cap securely over her babyish hair. "Papa is going down to the Palace Hotel to get rooms for all of us. Mrs. Conner is packing everything you'll need, and we'll have the best time. Your friends can come to see you and we'll all have tea in the Palm Court this afternoon."

Up and down the street, people were making themselves comfortable on their curbs, as if the occasion were a picnic. Most of the families had brought out furniture, and two of them had set up laundry stoves and their cooks were making coffee. Children were running and shouting happily, and the Verts' dog barked constantly.

"Is Mrs. Conner getting Mother's dress?" Jolie asked. She knew she sounded foolish, but she could not get the dress out of her mind. Mother loved it, and she would want it kept safe. But whatever had been in the bitter potion Jolie had been given was doing its work and her tongue felt thick.

"You mean the dress she wore last night?" Jane asked. "Mama told me about it."

"But is Mrs. Conner getting it out of the house? I want to take it to the hotel . . ."

Talking was too much effort. Jolie's breathing was easier now, but she was too tired to keep her eyes open.

In her sleep, she felt the next earthquake and the one after that. She heard herself say, "Mother?" Mrs. Conner smoothed her forehead and whispered, "Shh."

But then, later, Mrs. Conner suddenly exclaimed and Jolie sat up, wide-awake and staring around her. "What is it? What is it?"

In the south and west, the sky was boiling with black smoke. She heard a short, heavy thud, then another. A strange man talking with Mr. Vert said, "They're dynamiting buildings now, trying to stop the fires."

"What's burning?" Jolie asked as she tried to get up on one elbow.

"The whole of South of Market is burning," Mrs. Conner said. "But the fire department is handling it. There's nothing for us to worry about here. We're quite safe."

"Is my father back yet?"

"No, not yet. Close your eyes again. This will be over soon."

Jolie could not help herself from dozing, but sometimes she woke fully, with a start, always asking about her mother, always being told that there was no news yet, but everything would be fine. The men and older boys in the neighborhood took turns walking around, gathering news, reporting on the damage they could see. No one sounded worried—the boys often laughed.

Father came back once, just before eleven o'clock. He sat beside her silently, holding one of her hands so hard that he hurt her.

"Mother?" Jolie asked hoarsely.

He shook his head and then told her that her mother had died at the temporary hospital at the Mechanics Pavilion. Nothing could have been done to save her, not even if the emergency hospital had not been destroyed by the first earthquake.

"But what happened to her?" Jolie cried, unbelieving. "What happened?"

Dr. Logan hesitated, then said, "The kitchen china cupboard fell on her. She never knew what happened. She never woke up. She just slept—and then left us."

He sat with her for a while, weeping, holding her hands in both of his. "But she never awoke," he said again, as if that could be a consolation to her.

Through numb lips, Jolie asked, "Where is she now?"

Father blinked. "We took her to the cemetery. Friends are . . . well, she's being taken care of. Don't think about it."

Mrs. Conner, the Verts, and the other neighbors kept their distance while father and daughter sat together, until five minutes after eleven, when another quake struck. Father leaned over her, protecting her, and when it was done with them, he stood and said, "We're setting up a hospital at Golden Gate Park and I'm needed."

"But where will I find you?" Jolie cried, terrified at his leaving her. "Are you coming back here for me? Mr. Vert said we can't go to the Palace Hotel now because it's in the path of the fire. Should we go to the park to find you?"

"No, no," Father said. "You're safe enough here. Van Ness is only a block away, and it's too wide for the fire to cross. I'll come back—or send messages. There's no need to worry."

But Jolie could smell the smoke and see it rising hundreds of feet into the southern sky. Half the city was burning now. Hadn't he heard what she had heard? The earthquake had destroyed most of the city and the fire was consuming the wreckage, neighborhood by neighborhood.

"Yes, Father," she said. "I won't worry."

David Fairfield, young and tall and the owner of a fine automobile, waited for her father. He had appointed himself Father's driver, and he had been kind enough to stay away while she heard about her mother. Now he only nodded solemnly at her as Father climbed in beside him.

The Verts gathered around her. "We're very sorry," Mrs. Vert said. "Your mama was the loveliest, kindest person I ever knew."

Jolie's eyes swam with tears and she turned her face into the pillows.

Mrs. Conner, dressed in her usual black now, sat beside her. "Joseph heated soup and tea for you on the laundry stove. Don't disappoint him. He's heartbroken about your mama, and she would have shown him she appreciated his work by eating a good lunch."

Joseph, a small Chinese man who had renamed himself when he began working for the Logans, stood behind Mrs. Conner, holding a tray.

"Thank you, Joseph," she said as she struggled upright and accepted the tray. How could they expect her to eat? Did they understand what had happened to her?

The Verts' cook had fixed a meal, too. Jane brought her plate of scrambled eggs and bacon and sat on the curb next to her. "We're supposed to be brave," she said as she spread an embroidered linen napkin over her knees. "But I'd like to holler my head off, and if I were you, I would. My father says that this part of the city won't burn, but the fire is still spreading. Have you heard all the explosions? The soldiers are dynamiting houses everywhere to keep them from catching fire, but the dynamite is starting even more fires. And the soldiers on Market Street are herding people out into the side streets instead of letting them go where they want, to get away from the fires. And the soldiers even shot some looters. If you ask me, it serves them right."

Jolie looked down her street at the row of handsome houses, some not damaged at all. All the chimneys had fallen, of course, but otherwise one might not realize how bad the earthquakes had been. But the air was acrid from the smoke that rolled up from South of Market and the waterfront and Hayes Valley.

Mrs. Conner had another paper twist of bitter powder, and Jolie drank the potion willingly. She wanted to sleep and wake to find that the nightmare was over and Mother was sitting by her bed with the tea she had gone down to the kitchen to make.

"But Mother's dress," she murmured, ready to sleep.

Mrs. Conner bent over her again. "I packed it for you. You'll wear it yourself one day. And her diamond earrings, too, lovey."

Jolie's father came back once more, during the late afternoon, to check on her and assure her that she was in no danger. "The Verts will take care of you, and you have Mrs. Conner and Joseph, too."

"But I want to come with you," Jolie said.

"No, no, there are things going on at the hospital that you shouldn't see," he said. He glanced over at David, his driver, and back to her again. "You're luckier than others, Jolie. Most streets are jammed with thousands of refugees who have no place to go. Try to rest and I'll see you in the morning. You'll be quite safe here."

David was fidgeting behind the wheel of the automobile. The backseat was piled with boxes and bags, and Jolie recognized the names of two pharmacies. She was keeping Father from people who needed him.

"I'll see you in the morning," she told him reluctantly.

Jane plopped down beside her. "Why don't I read to

you for a while?" she asked. "I've halfway through *Love's Lost Song*, but I'll begin again for you."

"Your mother lets you read *that*?" Jolie asked. Her classmates at the Academy had been passing the book around—in a paper cover—last fall.

"No, she doesn't," Jane said, opening the book. "Listen, Jolie, this is how it starts. 'The ravishing Miss DuChamps arrived in London . . .'"

Another time, Jolie thought, she would have laughed aloud.

The families on the block behaved as if they were having a party. The men and the servants had dragged out everyone's dining room furniture, and the maids carried around food to share. The men had their drinks and cigars afterward while everyone sat on chairs in the street and watched the rest of the city burn. Occasionally a cloud of smoke and sparks swept over them, and the children would scream, running and laughing.

Jolie, propped up on her bed, watched them all and wondered if she had lost her mind.

Darkness fell, but the talking and laughter went on for a while before they died away, as the people tried to rest. Small children protested for a few minutes. Overhead, the sky was covered with a thick haze. South of Market, the smoke was heavy and copper colored, slashed with flames.

The dynamiting went on, and between the quick and heavy thuds, Jolie heard sounds from Van Ness Avenue, where she knew that hundreds of people were still walking, shuffling, struggling toward a place where they could safely rest. Soldiers had been posted there to keep them from stopping on that elegant street.

Were she and her neighbors were really safe? If not, where could *they* go? It seemed to her that all of the sky in the south and west was on fire now.

CHAPTER 3

Kate

THE KEELYS and the Flannerys joined the mass of silent refugees moving toward Market Street to escape the horror of the encroaching fires. But Market Street was jammed with quake victims dragging their baggage and children over heaps of debris, avoiding trolley tracks that had heaved up and tangles of fallen wires. Some wanted to reach the ferry dock, but others struggled in the opposite direction, looking for shelter and safety. Some still wore their nightclothes. A barefoot woman pushing a sewing machine picked her way along carefully, leaving bloody tracks. An old man followed her, carrying a houseplant and talking to himself. Everyone had something—clothing, bedding, bulging sacks, infants, pets, and, to Kate's astonishment, pianos and sofas.

Soldiers began roughly herding the refugees into the side streets north of Market, and Kate's party crossed over, but within a block, they lost track of their neighbors.

"Where will we go, Ma?" Ellen asked as she maneuvered the top-heavy baby buggy around a sofa that appeared to have fallen out of a ripped-open building.

Mrs. Flannery said, "To Union Square. We know people who will take us in."

"I don't see how I can go to the store this morning," Aunt Grace said as she hurried beside Kate. "But surely Mr. Koppler won't hold it against me."

Ellen barked a laugh. "Miss Keely, the department store is probably knocked flat and on fire," she said. "The floorwalker won't be looking to dock your pay."

Aunt Grace grabbed Kate's arm and squeezed it hard enough to make Kate wince. "I've lost my job, then," she murmured urgently. "Katie, what will we do?"

"We have bigger things to worry about now," Kate said grimly. Mrs. Flannery looked back at her and shook her head slightly. Aunt Grace did not see her expression.

"We're going to be just fine, all of us," Mrs. Flannery called out. "Come on, Joe, stop dawdling, or I'll have your hide before this day is out."

Joe laughed disrespectfully, but he lifted his end of the Keelys' trunk a little higher. Kate's hands were blistered, and she was thankful she had not found more things to put in their trunk.

"She'll never hide me," Joe confided in her. "Ma's never hided anybody."

"But I will," Ellen said. Hugh laughed shortly and winked at his sister.

A man walking nearby laughed, too, as if the comment had been directed at him. He went on laughing, and Kate saw that one side of his face was covered with blood and his eye was missing. A small girl walking with him said, "Dad, now Dad, please don't." The man stumbled and fell to his knees, and the girl burst into tears. An old woman stopped and bent over him, murmuring. The other refugees surged on.

At one corner, they passed a dead man and three dead horses, crushed under bricks. A snapping live wire hissed over them.

I don't believe what I'm seeing, Kate thought as she averted her eyes. I don't believe any of this. I'll wake up in my father's house, six years old again, with my parents still alive and sleeping down the hall, and my mother will come in and tell me about the green Irish fields unfolding clear to the sea that is the wild road leading to this magical America, this place where nothing bad ever happens.

This place where both my parents died. This place that has fallen around me and is on fire.

They set off again. The city was made of nothing but hills, Kate thought in despair. And we're always on the wrong side of every one. The trunk seemed to grow heavier. She was thirsty and her eyes burned. But everyone walking with them faced the same struggle, so she did not complain.

Union Square was crammed with worried refugees, exchanging rumors and fears in quiet voices. But the nearby damaged homes of Mrs. Flannery's friends were vacant.

"Now what?" Hugh asked his mother.

Mrs. Flannery looked around, hesitated, and then said, "Why, we'll just keep moving. We want to stay away from the fires South of Market."

Her children groaned and protested noisily. "I'd rather sit on the curb!" Ellen complained. "Ma! We've been walking forever, and we're tired and hungry."

But Mrs. Flannery looked back toward the south where the smoke rose and shook her head. "We have to keep moving." Kate looked back, too, and knew that by now their homes were burned, gone forever.

They went on, dragging their belongings. Once, behind them, they heard a gas main explode, and small bits of stone rained down on them. They passed a woman digging in ruins, while next door, where the front of a house had fallen away, a man sat on the edge of his second-floor bedroom and watched her dispassionately. Twice, ambulances rattled past them, with bloody bodies stacked inside.

Aunt Grace looked up at the heavy smoke boiling in the southern sky and said, "We'll have to start over again, just the way my parents did when they came here from Ireland, with nothing in their hands except a change of clothes and nothing in their pockets except holes."

There was a moment of silence, and then Mrs. Flannery laughed. "When I left Ireland, I had an English shilling that my father told me to throw overboard after I spit on it, but I forgot. I found the thing after I married, and I asked Himself what to do with it, and he said, "Let's see if it's worth anything here." And didn't he just find one of those people who collect coins, if you can believe that. We sold it for a hundred dollars—I swear that I'm telling the truth—and started building our first house, out in Cow Hollow, where we lived until he died, God rest him. Now wouldn't the English hate that story if they knew it."

"Do you have another shilling, Ma?" asked Hugh, grinning. "We can use it now."

"I'd rather have the hundred dollars," she said. "In silver. I've got a hunch that people will be thinking about money tomorrow, and them that has it will be thankful."

"We'll be fine, Ma," Hugh said.

"We'll all be fine," Kate added. But in her heart, she was terrified. She and her aunt had nothing except what was in their trunk, a few articles of clothing and photographs, and the change in Aunt Grace's pocketbook. Kate still wore her nightgown under her dress, and she felt through the fabric of her skirt to see if the photograph was still in her nightgown pocket. Yes.

"Someone will come along and tell us what to do," Aunt Grace said. "It's just a matter of time."

Another hill. Joe was in tears and begged to stop, and Aunt Grace was staggering in exhaustion, so they found a yard with a clear view of the burning city. Several people had spread blankets on the ground and were eating as calmly as if they were on a picnic in Golden Gate Park. Mrs. Flannery asked if anyone had water to spare, but no one did. The men had appealed at houses along the way, they said, but the story was the same everywhere. The water mains had been broken during the quakes and no one had water. There was not even water to fight the terrible fires.

Kate looked out over the ruined city, where the skeletons of buildings rose up in piles of burning rubble, and she realized that she could no longer identify the streets below her. And over it all, there was the black smoke with gushing flames at its core. Soldiers were dynamiting houses everywhere in an effort to stop the fires, and periodically explosions would send shattered, burning wood in all directions, spreading fires and setting off gas explosions. Market Street had been cleared of refugees, who surged through the side streets. The waterfront burned fiercely.

"The fire's crossed Market," Hugh said quietly behind her. "Look there."

She saw where the fire had spilled over the street. "Will it come up here?"

"Yes—there's nothing to stop it." Sparks whirled up like a cloud of angry insects from a block of houses that burned busily. The fire jumped an intersection, and houses on both sides of the next streets burst suddenly into flames that spun wildly and were sucked upward, shrieking. Kate saw three people running ahead of the fire, but they burst into balls of flame and vanished in the holocaust.

"Hugh, we shouldn't stay here," she said urgently.

"We can't keep hauling all our stuff," he said. "It slows us down too much. Have you seen all the trunks people left in the street? We should take only what we need."

She knew Hugh was right. He spoke to his mother for a moment, and then they began going through their possessions.

Aunt Grace looked at Kate as if she had forgotten until that instant what Kate was wearing. "You need to put on a petticoat and drawers," she hissed behind her hand. "And you could get a shirtwaist under the dress easily enough. We can't leave everything behind. You can change behind that old fence, and I'll hold up the blanket."

"It doesn't matter ..." Kate began. She hated the idea of putting clean clothes on when she was dirty. She needed to wash! But below them, the world was burning.

"If you're wearing it, you don't have to carry it," Mrs. Flannery called out.

She was right. Kate, shielded by the fence and blanket, changed clothes hurriedly, putting on a dress over a shirtwaist and skirt. Aunt Grace buttoned herself into a jacket and then a coat, and stuffed all the pockets with undergarments and handkerchiefs. Kate tied the photograph album into a thin old towel, then pulled on a knitted jacket that had belonged to her mother. "We look like vagrants," she said.

"And we are," Ellen observed sourly. She had succeeded in hooking a second dress closed over the one she wore. Joe laughed and joked until Hugh silenced him abruptly and warned him that there would be plenty of time to act like a fool, when they reached a place where they could count on being safe.

The families agreed that the small wagon should carry

bedding and dishes, because wherever they went, they would need those things. Everything else, including the portrait of Mr. Flannery, would have to be left behind. The Flannerys ceremoniously unwrapped the portrait and turned it to face the burning city, "just so he can see that what he predicted came to pass," Mrs. Flannery said.

They left the hill then, walking through blocks where ruined houses sat beside houses that seemed scarcely touched. Overhead, the smoke rose and the air was hard to breathe. They stopped often to talk to other people, exchanging news. Yes, the dynamiting would go on until the fire stopped, even though it seemed to cause even more fires. Looters had been shot. The city was— or was not—under martial law, depending upon the speaker. There was no hope of getting on a ferry, because everyone else was trying to get to Oakland, too. More troops had been sent in, and sailors, too.

They passed people who had built small stoves out of bricks so they could make coffee and cook eggs. Mrs. Flannery and Aunt Grace asked over and over where the people had found the food, and often it was food the people had brought from home. The grocery stores they passed were sold out.

"I'd wish I were dead if it wasn't a mortal sin," Mrs. Flannery said disgustedly. "I had a kitchen full of food, and all I took was bread."

"We had bacon," Aunt Grace said. "And biscuits."

"We'll find something," Kate said. "There has to be food somewhere."

Late in the afternoon they found one small store still open and they hurried inside to join the short line at the counter. There was a basket of eggs on a table behind the counter and two shelves still lined with canned goods. They could build their own stove, Hugh assured them, and cook eggs, and maybe the man even had bacon. Kate's mouth watered while she listened.

The grocer shoved canned goods across the wood counter and accepted money from a middle-aged woman wearing a fur-trimmed cape over a dressing gown. Mrs. Flannery's turn was next. "How much for a dozen eggs?" she asked the man.

"Eggs, one dollar each," the man said. He smiled, showing crooked teeth.

The Flannerys and Keelys had already counted the money they had between them, exactly eight dollars and fifty cents. Kate's ears rang. A dollar for each egg?

Mrs. Flannery was outraged. "I'd lay an egg myself before I'd pay *you* a dollar for one!" she shouted. "Shame on you, taking advantage of people at a time like this! For shame!"

The man shrugged. "If you don't buy them, somebody else will," he said. "If you're not customers, then get out."

Five people were standing in line behind them and no one was complaining about the price of the eggs. Mrs. Flannery sighed. "All right, ye thief. What have you got that decent people can afford to eat?"

"Bread, one dollar. Canned fruit, one dollar. Bacon, five dollars a pound. Soda pop . . ." the man recited.

"Ma!" Ellen implored. "Can't we get something? A couple of eggs cooked with the last of our bread and maybe a can of peaches? And some soda pop?"

"We should get the fruit at least," Aunt Grace said. "And something to drink."

They bought four cans of peaches, and seven bottles of soda pop. "We'd better enjoy this meal," Mrs. Flannery said as they moved half a block away. "Unless there's a miracle, we'll be hungry tomorrow."

They found room in a crowded park, no larger than a block square, and sat down to share their meal. Hugh opened the cans with his pocketknife and Mrs. Flannery produced a variety of saucers and small bowls from the wagon, along with several mismatched spoons. Kate quenched her thirst first, with soda pop tasting more delicious than anything she could have imagined. Aunt Grace ate only half her share of the peaches and passed the rest to Kate, swearing she was too nervous to eat.

"Why doesn't someone come along and tell us what we should be doing?" she complained. "We see soldiers, but they don't say anything except, 'Get over there. No, not there, over here.'"

Mrs. Flannery burst out laughing. "I expect we're lucky we haven't been shot by them. It's too much to expect that they've got the answers to our questions yet. Things will be better tomorrow, dearie."

Nearby, someone had used bedding to make a tent to shelter two sick children. Their mother had built a small fire and was boiling water she had found in a hole in a nearby street. Four men played cards on a blanket spread on the ground while children crawled over them, laughing. A woman cried constantly, wiping her face with the hem of her dress as she sat with her back against a trunk. A man with burned hands murmured reassuringly to her.

Kate wondered if they were going to sleep there that night. She was afraid to ask, wishing she shared her aunt's hope that eventually someone would come along and solve their problems.

Someone came along, but only to make everything worse. They had just finished their meal when an auto-mobile pulled up in the street and five soldiers got out. "Men, line up here! We need you to clear the streets. Men! All of you, get over here!"

No one moved. No one said a word. All across the small park, the shocked people stared, amazed.

"I'm telling you, line up here or you'll be shot!" the man yelled furiously. "This is an order!"

Kate gasped and stared around. Slowly, two men got to their feet, but they did not move toward the soldiers. Instead, they stood helplessly, their hands dangling, looking around as if someone could explain all of this.

The soldiers raised their rifles on command.

More men got to their feet now. A woman cried out, "Don't, Jerry! Don't go with them."

Slowly, slowly, men moved toward the automobile and the soldiers with their rifles held to their shoulders. The yelling man pointed to the man with burned hands and shouted at him to get in line. An old man with a cane made his way toward the soldiers, but one of them laughed and gestured to him to get back.

The yelling man saw Hugh. "What's wrong with you, sonny? Act like a man and get in line."

"No, Hugh!" Mrs. Flannery cried, reaching for his arm. Hugh got to his feet and she rose with him. "He's only fourteen!" she shouted. "He's only a boy!"

"He's old enough to pile bricks when he's told to!" the man yelled back.

Hugh walked toward him stiffly, and his mother followed, tripping over her skirt and staggering a few steps. "You can't take him!" she cried. "I won't find him again! I won't find him in all the crowds!"

Kate watched, frozen. Ellen rushed after her mother. "No, no," Aunt Grace whispered as she, too, got to her feet. "We can't allow this. We cannot allow this!"

Another young boy was directed to get into line with the men. And then another. Mrs. Flannery begged the yelling man, but he pulled a revolver from a holster and pointed it at her.

"Mama!" Ellen screamed. "Let him go! Let Hugh go!"

Suddenly, without warning, Joe picked up a rock and threw it at the yelling soldier. Aunt Grace grabbed him and yanked him behind her.

"They'll kill your mother," she said. "Is that what you want?"

The rock had hit the yelling man's chest. For a long moment he stood there, his revolver pointing at Mrs. Flannery. Hugh cried out, "I'm going with you! I'm going! Don't hurt her!"

The yelling man turned, laughed shortly, and walked away. Mrs. Flannery collapsed to her knees while Ellen burst into noisy tears.

Kate looked up at the smoky sky. Is anyone coming

to help us? she wondered. Does anyone anywhere care what is happening here? Beside her, Aunt Grace whispered, "I must go get Mrs. Flannery. I must get her right now, before something bad happens. Men . . . when they get like that . . . you don't know what they'll do. *I have to go now.*"

"*I'll* go," Kate said.

"You stay with Joe," Aunt Grace said. She straightened herself to stand as tall as she could and marched toward Mrs. Flannery and the soldiers with their guns. Everyone in the park watched the fragile woman. Kate held her breath, terrified, not knowing what might happen next.

When Aunt Grace reached her friend, Kate heard her say, "Stand up and come with me now, Mary Flannery. *This is the only way.*"

Mrs. Flannery rose unsteadily to her feet and watched Hugh disappear with the men and the soldiers. "My god," she said. "What if I can't find him again? He's only a boy."

"You'll find him," Aunt Grace said. "He'll be all right, and he'll be back soon. Before dark! You'll see."

"We'll wait here so he can find us," Mrs. Flannery babbled. "We can't be separated. The family must stay together."

"Of course," Aunt Grace said. "He'll be back before dark."

But the men and boys did not return. Mysteriously, in a way that Kate could not sort out, Mrs. Flannery and her aunt exchanged roles. Mrs. Flannery had been their guide, their firm support, throughout the whole terrible day. But now Aunt Grace became the one who made quiet, firm decisions that affected them all. She directed Ellen and Joe where to put out blankets and coats for Mrs. Flannery to lie down. She was the one who pointed out that the rest of them should take turns sitting up, in case there was news of some kind that might affect them. Or in case the fires spread too near.

Kate was awake most of the night, watching the ugly purple glow spreading in the sky, wondering where Hugh was, and listening to Mrs. Flannery's rosary beads clicking. A woman a few feet away had said that she thought the men would be kept until the whole city was cleared. But that could not be true, Kate thought. Mrs. Flannery, their strength, had begun to collapse when Hugh was taken away. What would happen if he did not come back?

Shortly after dawn, different soldiers came, this time to clear the park. The fire was growing close. The refugees had to leave, now, now!

Mrs. Flannery joined several other women, begging the soldiers for information about the men who had been taken away. Where were they? How would they be reunited?

But those soldiers knew nothing about the men and boys who had been marched away at gunpoint the afternoon before. Yes, the streets were being cleared of rubble. People were gathering in the parks and cemeteries, if they were not leaving the city by ferry.

"You'll find the men," a soldier told them roughly. "Get your things together and start walking. You can't stay here."

Silently, the people in the park left, walking ahead of the soldiers who herded them like cattle for several blocks before leaving them on their own.

"Where should we go?" Kate asked Mrs. Flannery and her aunt.

But Mrs. Flannery did not hear her. "Hugh," she whispered as she looked back over her shoulder.

"We'll go toward Van Ness," Aunt Grace said loudly, firmly. "Other people have gone that way. We can cross it and get out of the way of the fire, and then we can decide what to do next."

Mrs. Flannery did not answer, and she only moved because Ellen pulled her by the arm. They followed Aunt Grace—and the fire followed them, relentlessly.

CHAPTER 4

Jolie

THERE WAS no real dawn on the morning after the earthquake. All night, the sky had burned a dull copper color above the burning city, and in the morning it looked dirty gray, while thick black smoke covered the sun.

Joseph left, explaining that he wanted to find his family. Chinatown had burned to the ground the day before, and many refugees were staying in the large parks. He apologized over and over again, even turning once when he was half a block away, so formal in his good black suit, to bow several times.

"I hope his parents are all right," Mrs. Conner said. "I told him to look for your father at Golden Gate Park and tell him what he finds out. Once he's relieved his mind, he can help out at the hospital. Goodness knows I can do whatever cooking we need until things are sorted out here."

Jolie said, "I want to find Father. I'm much better this morning, and Golden Gate Park isn't that far away. We'll have to leave here anyway. The fires are getting closer." She had not slept much during the night, and dreamed again that her mother was standing over her, wearing her beautiful Worth dress, and holding a cup of tea. Waking had been a bitter disappointment.

"The park is much too far for you to walk," Mrs. Conner said. She would have tucked her blanket in around her, but Jolie protested.

"I'm going to get dressed now," she said. "I'm embarrassed, lying here in my nightdress."

"You can dress, but that's all," Mrs. Conner said firmly. "You'll come right back and lie down again. You're a sick girl, and going through all this is making you sicker."

"I'm fine," Jolie lied. Grief and fear left her exhausted, and the pains in her legs were worse. But this was a dangerous time to be ill. It did not take much imagination to see that any physical disability put one at even more risk. The maid brought clothes for Jolie, and she and the housekeeper held up blankets while Jolie dressed hurriedly in a cotton skirt and shirt.

They had heard that Van Ness Avenue had been crowded with refugees, but soldiers had brought up cannons and were going to blow up the houses that they had not yet dynamited. The homeless had begun crowding into the Logans' street by eight o'clock, and Jolie watched, unbelieving, as hundreds of people trudged past her.

Where had they spent the night? Most of them were grimy from smoke and soot, and all of them carried things—sacks and suitcases and boxes. Some even dragged trunks behind them. One young man had mounted a trunk on skates.

Many of the women obviously were wearing several dresses, and one had three hats perched on her head, each one drooping different colored feathers. Some of the young people seemed astonishingly cheerful, considering that they were keeping ahead of a fire that might catch up with them soon enough. Jolie heard girls her own age laughing as they passed.

But others were haggard and somber, wearing sorrow on their faces. Some led friends or relatives who seemed almost stunned. Many people wore bloody bandages made of strips of clothing or rags.

Often, people stopped to ask the residents on the street for water, but there was none to be had. Sometimes they slowed as they passed the little stoves where cooks fried eggs and bacon. A few people asked for food and received whatever the family could spare. It was a strange sight for Jolie, seeing the refugees filing down the street while neighbors watched them go past as they ate, as if the parade had little or nothing to do with them.

Mrs. Conner and Jane sat beside Jolie, offering occasional amazed comments at the sights. Jane was fascinated with what the refugees carried, but Mrs. Conner worried about where they were going and how they would find food.

A red-haired girl passed, her arm around a middle-aged woman who stumbled frequently. That marvelous thick, braided hair! Jolie sighed, almost envious. But she would not change places with her, not even for her hair. Another woman walked with them. She seemed stunned by events, for she never raised her head. A boy followed them, complaining noisily about having to pull a wagon by himself, since somebody named Hugh wasn't there to help. The red-haired girl turned on him suddenly and cried, "Joe, hush your mouth." A tall, dark girl walking behind the boy laughed and called, "Give him a smack, Kate."

"I believe I know that woman," Mrs. Conner said slowly, but the crowd closed around the family and it disappeared. "God bless them."

"Should we call them back?" Jolie asked.

Mrs. Conner shook her head. "We can't help them. They need water and a safe place, and we don't have either one."

Up and down the street, a few families whose automobiles had not yet been confiscated were preparing to leave. The fires were getting too close.

At noon, David Fairfield returned. He had a pass on his windshield now, to prevent soldiers from taking his car and putting him to work cleaning earthquake debris off the main streets. He had discarded his jacket somewhere, and his shirt was sooty and stained with what Jolie thought must surely be blood.

"Is my father all right?" she called out before he had time to reach her.

"He's fine," David told her. "He's sent me to ask the

Verts to take you to the Prescotts' boat. It's docked near Fort Warden—Mr. Vert knows exactly where. They have enough room for all of you, but you must go now, to Oakland. If the fire doesn't stop at Van Ness . . ."

Jolie shook her head vehemently. "I want to be with my father. How will I find him again if I go to Oakland? Look at all these people! How will I find him?"

"He'll find you!" David said. "He'll come to Oakland when this is all over."

"No," Jolie said. "No! I want to be with my father."

Three men had stopped by David's car, watching him closely. One of them suddenly climbed in the front seat. David and Mr. Vert ran toward them, shouting. The two other men reached in the back, tugging at the boxes of medical supplies stacked there. David grabbed the one behind the steering wheel and threw him into the street. Mr. Vert picked up a brick and threatened the man nearest him with it. "Leave the supplies alone!" he shouted. "They're for the hospital! Take your hands off of them!"

"Pa!" Jane screamed.

There was a moment when everyone seemed to freeze in place. And then, suddenly, the nearest neighbors converged on the automobile and pulled the men away from it.

"I have to leave," David told Jolie as he got behind the wheel. "Do what your father says, Jolie. You'll be safe in Oakland." He drove away, honking to clear people from his path.

"All right, let's get out of here," Mr. Vert said. "Children, get in the auto. Hurry, now. The Prescotts are waiting for us. Jolie, you're next. Get some of your belongings and sit next to Jane."

The Verts scrambled into the car with their nervous dog and their luggage, but Jolie stepped back hastily. "I can't," she said, nearly blind with panic. "I have to find my father. Take Mrs. Conner in my place."

"Jolie!" Mrs. Conner said sharply. "Get in the backseat and do as you're told."

"I will not!" Jolie said. "I am going to the park to find Father."

But Mr. Vert was not listening to them argue. His car lurched into the street, nearly hitting a man holding a small child, and disappeared into the crowd.

"I wish you'd given some consideration to how you're planning on getting anywhere on your own two feet," Mrs. Conner told Jolie. "Because it won't be very far. Not with your heart."

"I'll walk to the park, Mrs. Conner," Jolie said. "With or without you. But you are my friend, and I would rather have you by my side."

Mrs. Conner met her gaze steadily for a moment, and then she began to weep. "You remind me of your mother," she said brokenly. "What will we do without her?"

Mrs. Conner and the maid repacked the suitcases, so that there were enough essentials in two of them to maintain the three women for a long weekend. At Jolie's almost hysterical insistence, her mother's Worth dress was included in the one Mrs. Conner would carry. Obviously they would need food, so Mrs. Conner brought bread and canned goods from the ruined kitchen, but the suitcases were even heavier then.

"The photographs!" Jolie cried suddenly. "We forgot them. We have to bring them with us."

Soldiers were walking down the street, shouting at the refugees. "Clear the street! Move on! Clear the street!" People began hurrying, avoiding looking at the soldiers, as if they had been through this before and feared what might happen if they appeared to hesitate. As soon as they reached a corner, they turned north. In only a few minutes, the street was clear.

"I'll run in and get the box of photographs," Mrs. Conner said. "It won't take but a minute . . ."

But a soldier gestured to her. "Stop! You aren't allowed to go back in the house. It's not safe."

"I was just in there!" she protested. "It's safe. I only want to get one thing—"

"Stay away from the house!" the man shouted.

Mrs. Conner hesitated. Farther down the street, a soldier kicked in the door of the Parsons' house. "What's that man doing?" she said.

"Clear the street now!" the soldier yelled angrily. "Get moving, all three of you."

"Let's go!" the maid said. "They're shooting people all over the city."

"I only want the family photographs . . ." Mrs. Conner began again, but the soldier took a long step toward her and she stopped talking, picked up one of the suitcases, and took Jolie's hand. "Come on now. Don't look back. Your father will straighten everything out, as soon as we tell him."

The two of them, with the maid straggling behind and whining, walked in the direction the refugees had taken. Jolie looked back once and saw two of the soldiers entering her house. Oh, Mother, she thought, what would you think of all this?

They joined the march of refugees one block over. Most were heading toward Golden Gate Park, where some said there was food available and perhaps even tents had been set up. Jolie walked steadily, refusing to acknowledge pain or breathlessness, and when Mrs. Conner asked her how she felt, she assured the woman that she felt well. It helped her to say it aloud. After all, she was better off than many of the people on the street. She was not injured. She was not even carrying a heavy load of clothing. For a while she kept pace with a woman holding a small, staring baby.

"It's his first earthquake," the woman said cheerfully. "We were supposed to move to Portland last month, but I begged my husband to stay until Will was three months old, and now look what I did." She laughed, as if the whole catastrophe were nothing more than a prank.

"Where is your husband now?" Mrs. Conner asked.

"Oh, they recruited him to help clear Market Street, although I don't know why. The whole place either fell down or is on fire now. He'll have plenty to tell us when he catches up with us."

"Aren't you worried that you won't find him?" Jolie asked. She was wheezing slightly and Mrs. Conner looked at her sharply.

"How many places can we go?" the woman said. "The parks or Oakland. He'll find us."

The middle of the street was crowded with refugees, and the curbs lined with people resting. Some would get to their feet and stagger on, and others would hurry to take their places. It seemed to Jolie that she could not remember clearly her mother's face or what their home had been like only two days before. We must go back to the house when this is over, she told herself. Everything about Mother is in that house. We must go back.

They stopped once for a few minutes, in a yard where a wall had collapsed, and ate bread and cheese, washing the food down with the warm soda. Jolie had difficulty getting to her feet again, and Mrs. Conner tried to push her down. "I'll find a better place for you somewhere," she said. "You càn sit here and wait."

"Don't leave me behind!" Jolie cried, close to tears. "Promise me that you won't leave me behind!" Mrs. Conner helped her to her feet, and they moved on, slowly.

Fires burned on three sides of them, and sometimes ashes and sparks poured down on them. The sun loomed sickly through thick orange pall and the air stank of everything that could burn in a city—wood and cloth and paper and manure and human flesh and animal hair and even metal. Several people walking with them spoke of seeing metal rails melting like water and stones burning. "People are burning to ashes, even their bones," a man said tiredly. "We'll never know how many have died."

"There's food in the park," people said over and over. "There's water. We'll have tents to sleep in tonight." Jolie believed none of it. She knew that she would stumble on forever, her heart pounding, her knees swelling, and worst of all, her mother was dead and she would never see her again. This was what hell was like. This *was* hell.

Jolie realized suddenly that the maid was no longer behind them. But she had not taken the suitcase with Mother's dress in it. Nothing else mattered.

When they reached the Panhandle, the entrance to the park, they saw a billboard covered with writing, messages left by refugees trying to locate their relatives. But Jolie knew where her father was, at the temporary hospital in the park. All she had to do was walk a little longer, a little farther. She pushed her glasses back up on her nose and concentrated on staying on her feet. I can do this, she thought. I'll do this because someday I'm going back to my mother's house to live there again, and everything will be just the way it always was.

The hospital was easy to find. The lines of injured people were long, and Mrs. Conner tried to lead Jolie past a table near the entrance, where three men sat, interviewing the victims. One man called out to her to stop and get to the end of the line. Jolie, exhausted, felt her knees nearly giving way.

"This is Dr. Logan's daughter," Mrs. Conner said. "He'll want to see her. She's walked all this way and she's very ill."

The man hesitated. A man nearby said, "I don't care who she is, she waits in line just like the rest of us."

But David came through the crowd then, carrying blankets, and saw her. "Jolie," he said, shocked.

She fainted.

The first night, she slept in a tent near the surgery, so that her father could watch her. The next morning, she and Mrs. Conner were moved to a small tent farther away. Sometimes Mrs. Conner was gone for a long time, but Jolie dozed, hardly aware of anything. When the housekeeper came back, she always had a bit of food or hot tea or fruit. She had found friends there, two families from the block, and a number of the servants. Joseph was there, with his mother and sister, she told Jolie. He would cook her a meal as soon as he could, he had promised.

Jolie thought of her mother, wept often, and slept, dreaming of the house.

She woke once to hear voices next to the tent.

"It's so hot," a young woman complained. "My eyes still burn from the ashes. How do you stand it?"

"I keep remembering what my mother told me about Ireland," another voice said. "How the green fields unfold and unfold to the cliffs and then the sea beyond. It sounds cool."

"It sounds like heaven," the first woman said. "Cool and green and quiet."

"Yes. Someday I'll go there and see for myself. I'll see everything that my mother saw. And I'll never come back here. Never!"

Jolie closed her eyes again and slept, to dream of her mother in her beautiful gray dress.

Part Two

Road Rise Up

1907

CHAPTER 5

Kate

SHORTLY AFTER nine on a foggy July morning, Kate hesitated at the boardinghouse door, pressing her fingers against her mouth. How can I explain to Aunt Grace? she thought. This is terrible. What are we going to do now?

The door opened suddenly, startling her. "Katie?" Mrs. Flannery was on her way out, dressed for grocery shopping in a dark blue coat and wide-brimmed black hat. "Dearie, what are you doing back home again? You're still sick, aren't you? We never should have let you try to go to work today."

It would have been so easy to lie and tell Mrs. Flannery that she had come home because the cough from her bad summer cold was still hanging on. But the truth would be obvious soon enough.

"The supervisor fired me because I missed four days," Kate said, struggling to hold back angry tears at the memory. She had climbed that wretched long flight of wooden steps from the back of the hardware store to the loft, only to have been met by Miss Thatcher and told that she had been replaced "with someone who appreciates the work more than you. And I never did believe that you were sixteen, missy!" Sick for four days and then fired!

Mrs. Flannery did not need to hear the details from Kate. "Sakes," she muttered as she gathered Kate into her arms. "There's no mercy in this world for women, not even from other women. Go inside and get back into your dressing gown. Ellen and your aunt are still in the kitchen and they'll fix a cup of tea for you. And don't worry about anything. After everything we've been through this last year, you know that things will work out, one way or another!"

Katie went inside, humiliated and longing for a way to avoid telling her aunt the bad news. Aunt Grace had been on crutches since the year before. Her job with a department store had been lost when the earthquake destroyed the building, and finding another position had been out of the question because of her condition, so Katie had not returned to high school. She had worked for a plumbing shop first, but the makeshift building had burned to the ground when the poorly installed gas line had exploded one night. For the next ten months she had worked for the hardware store, but now that was lost, too. The small amount of insurance money Aunt Grace had received for their belongings, destroyed in the fire, had mostly gone to help Mrs. Flannery purchase the boardinghouse. They had eighteen paying boarders, so the enterprise was a success. But everyone had to share the other expenses, and now Kate had lost her job.

She crept quietly up the front stairs to the bedroom she and her aunt shared and flopped facedown on her bed, not caring that she was wrinkling her best summer coat. She had hated the job anyway, hated the smells of rubber and tar that drifted up from the main floor, hated the other women in the office who had seemed so crude and overbearing, and most of all, she had hated the frizzy-haired Miss Thatcher. Miss Thatcher with her sneers and pompous airs and shirtwaists that were never quite clean! Kate sat up, pounded her pillow several times, and said aloud the shocking word Hugh had used with such satisfaction when describing his own employer—before his mother fined him ten cents and made him clean the roof gutters.

Slightly satisfied, she set about removing her office clothes. The simple, stylish homemade dress had twenty-five hooks on and under the bodice, and she had put in every one of them, something she regretted every morning when she faced them again. Her cotton dressing gown was too flimsy for such a cool morning, so she wrapped herself in the flowered shawl Ellen had given to her for her fifteenth birthday. As she went downstairs to join the women in the kitchen, she let down her long red hair and sighed with guilty pleasure. It was good to be home on a cold and foggy San Francisco morning.

"I lost my job," she announced immediately when

she walked into the large, bright room that always smelled of good cooking.

"God in heaven!" exclaimed Mary Clare, the cook, who dropped the towel she held and rushed to Kate to hug her so hard that Kate could barely get her breath. "You spurned one of them men in the sales department, didn't ye?" Mary Clare was passionately fond of the romance novels penned by Mrs. A. J. Hightower and Mrs. Flora Delistrada. Kate and Ellen laughed at them, but read them whenever Mary Clare was finished with them.

"No, Miss Thatcher spurned me," Kate said bitterly. "She replaced me with someone she said would appreciate the work more than I did—by never getting sick. And she found out I'm not sixteen. It's the only place in the city that won't hire people under sixteen."

"And this wonderful new employee has promised faithfully never to catch a cold?" Ellen asked interestedly, leaning on her elbows at the big kitchen table. "I'll bet she's one of those people who comes to work and coughs all over everybody else, and then brags that she has never lost a day of work because she makes a novena to St. Jude every year." Ellen, too, was between jobs, having lost a position in a department store modeling frocks for wealthy women after she complained that she did not like to be "picked at by fat women who could not fit into a smart gown even if a tent canvas was added to the back seam."

"Miss Thatcher seems to think the new girl can keep her promise." Kate slid into the chair next to her aunt. "Auntie, I'm so sorry. I'll find something else. You know everybody is desperate to find workers. Please don't start worrying."

"I'm not worried," Aunt Grace said firmly as she took a clean cup and saucer for Kate from the sideboard and hobbled back to the table. "I haven't worried about anything since that cornice fell on me in the aftershock. If that didn't kill me, nothing will. You'll have a wonderful job in no time at all."

"Listen, Ma's raising the rent on the McCarthy boys because they come in so late and make so much racket," Ellen offered. "They agreed, too. Anything rather than giving up the parties. So we're in wonderful shape—right now, anyway."

"And you and I will find jobs in one of the new buildings on Market Street and have offices of our own and typewriters—" Kate began.

"That would kill me," Ellen said flatly. "I believe I really would die, shut up in an office with all those stuffy old maids."

Ellen was dark and beautiful, and everywhere she went men stared and smiled. Kate both envied and admired her. Ellen had modeled gowns from Paris, and once had been sent flowers by a wealthy admirer, but Mrs. Flannery had returned the flowers to his home in person and presented them to the man's wife with a crisp explanation. The women in the boardinghouse never tired of discussing the occasion—and the aftermath.

"Then what will you do?" asked Mary Clare as she filled Kate's cup and then refilled the others on the table.

"I was talking to Mrs. McFee's Mary—you know,

the older daughter who works in a theater—and she says they're looking for girls to take care of the costumes. Girls who can use a sewing machine."

Kate leaned forward with interest. "I could do that."

"No, you could not," Aunt Grace said firmly. "You're just a child. I don't want you anywhere around those theater people. Heavens, what a thought."

"But I know a lot about sewing," Kate complained. "Look at all the things I've made since I got the sewing machine." A boarder had left in the middle of the night, still owing rent, and had left behind a sewing machine, which Kate had appropriated joyfully.

"You're a wonderful seamstress," Ellen said generously. "It would suit her perfectly, Miss Keely. She's clever with a bolt of cloth—even if she doesn't have any style."

Kate laughed and choked on her tea. "Oh, thank you so very much, Miss Flannery."

"Well, you don't have *real* style," Ellen said, laughing. "You dress like a schoolteacher."

"Which was what I wanted to be one day," Kate said.

"Oh, dear, I'm sorry, Kate," Aunt Grace said. "If it hadn't been for me—"

"If it hadn't been for you, I'd have been put in an orphanage when my father died," Kate said firmly. "As Father O'Brien says, we're all exactly where we're supposed to be."

But in her heart she did not believe it. She was meant to be in Ireland, Ireland, Ireland, where the green fields unfolded to the sea. She was not meant to stay in this burned-out, half-rebuilt city surrounded by ugly brown hills, with the dirt blowing in the summer streets, and horses that had been worked to death lying by the curbs every single day. She hated it so much! She suddenly burst into tears and put her head down on the table.

"Ah, lovey, don't cry," Mary Clare cried, weeping along with her. "It'll all come right, you'll see."

"It'll come right when we make it come right," Kate said bitterly. She raised her head and wiped her eyes on a corner of the shawl. "And not a minute before."

While San Francisco was springing up around her, renewed and strong, Kate's spirits had withered. She still had nightmares about the earthquake and fire. Leaving high school so abruptly had cast her, unprepared, into a working world she had not imagined. Ellen, cynical and amused, moved from one job to another with a shrug and a laugh. Ellen's brother Hugh, impressed into street clearing after the quake, had gone to work first for a company rebuilding the streets and then for a company building skyscrapers. He was barely sixteen, looked older, and was saving most of his earnings so that he could go into business for himself and take care of his mother, sister, and younger brother. All of the boarders worked and seemed contented, but Kate could not find her happiness. She wanted to return to school, but that opportunity was lost to her, probably forever. And the city that demanded and received the loyalty of the others was, for Kate, haunted. She wanted to leave it, but that was impossible, too.

The women lingered in the kitchen, occasionally rising to help Mary Clare with lunch preparations before returning to their teacups. It was the times like these that Kate loved best, when the women in the house sat together in the kitchen. Ellen supplied delicious gossip about San Francisco's wealthy families, while Mary Clare entertained them with her tales of Ireland, where she had been the eldest of thirteen children and ran barefoot until her confirmation, "When the bishop would not confirm ennybody who had no shoes, and didn't I wear my Gran's, and her with feet half the size of mine, and didn't I pull them off the minute I got outside so I could run home cooling me feet in the rain. That was a sweet day, not mean and dusty like the days are here." In her imagination, Kate saw that sweet day, with gentle, cool rain falling, and a big family gathering around a meal later on.

Mrs. Flannery returned, red-faced and cheerful, with her string bags filled with fresh vegetables and an enormous beef roast.

"You'll never guess who I saw at the market," she said as she removed her hat and coat and hung them on the rack in the corner. "I wasn't sure she was still in San Francisco, after the quake and all, and her losing her lady that she had loved and worked for all those years. But there she was—"

"Ma, who are you talking about?" Ellen demanded impatiently.

"Why, Mrs. Conner, who else?" her mother replied. "She who worked for Dr. Logan, whose wife was killed in the earthquake, and doesn't his daughter have heart disease, poor child."

"Heart disease?" Mary Clare asked suspiciously as she poured tea for her employer. "That's not catching, is it?"

Mrs. Flannery shook her head. "Of course not. No,

no, the poor girl got scarlet fever the winter before the quake, and it gave her heart trouble and bad legs."

"Poor kid," Ellen said thoughtfully. "How old is she?"

"Why, she's only seventeen." Mrs. Flannery helped herself to half a thick slice of bread and spread butter on it.

"Seventeen!" Ellen scoffed. "You made her sound like a baby."

"She *is* a baby," Mrs. Flannery said. "Mrs. Conner said she only got out of her wheelchair last week, when she moved back to the city. She and Mrs. Conner have been living over there in Marin County in all the fresh air with only two day maids to help out."

"Two maids?" Ellen asked, suddenly cross. "Nice for her, being in the country while the rest of us choke to death on the dust and go deaf from the noise. Why did she come back?"

"Oh, she insisted on coming back to the city. She's got a passion for the house her mother died in," Mrs. Flannery said. "Mary Clare, do I see potatoes soaking in that pot? You're boiling them for lunch? I thought you were frying them."

"What passion?" Aunt Grace asked, alarmed. "That doesn't sound nice."

"Well, that's what Dr. Logan calls it. A passion for the house where her mother died. So he's had it repaired, and now it's exactly like it was, just to suit the girl, although he really wanted to send her to Ireland to stay with her rich aunt so she could get over her mother's death."

Ireland. The word rang like a silver bell in Kate's mind. "She doesn't want to go to Ireland?" she asked, amazed.

"Oh, she won't have it. She wants her past back again, Mrs. Conner says."

"Well, I'm just going to burst into tears over that sad story, Ma," Ellen said disrespectfully, and she laughed. "Imagine having problems like that. Shall she live in San Francisco in a mansion or shall she live in Ireland with her rich aunt? God give me a problem like that."

Mrs. Flannery smiled at her daughter. "Oh, it's a problem, all right, missy. And it's yours for the asking," she said.

Everybody stared at her. "What are you talking about, Ma?" Ellen asked.

Mrs. Flannery settled herself more comfortably on her chair. "There's only Mrs. Conner and the Chinese cook and his nephew in the house right now. They had a couple of Spanish maids who only stayed for a few weeks, even though there's not much work around the place. And then the doctor hired a Swedish lady—"

"Ma, what does this have to do with me?" Ellen said, her voice raising impatiently.

"The doctor wants a sort of companion for his daughter, somebody closer to her own age, who'll be handy around the house and go around town with her when she's well enough to visit her friends."

"You want me to be a *maid*?" Ellen exclaimed. "Ma! Never in a million years."

"He's going to pay forty dollars a month," Mrs. Flannery said.

The women stared at one another. "Forty dollars for a maid?" Aunt Grace asked.

Mary Clare's eyes brightened, but Mrs. Flannery said

sharply, "Dearie, the doctor is looking for a companion, someone who can fit in with the girl's crowd and maybe go to Ireland with her as soon as she can travel."

Stout Mary Clare's gray hair seemed to droop even more, and she sighed. "That wouldn't be me."

"So *now* what do you think?" Mrs. Flannery asked her daughter. "Good pay and a chance to meet the nicest people in San Francisco."

"I would rather die than be a maid. And I already know that crowd, Ma! Haven't I been snubbed a million times already by them? 'Turn this way, miss. No, turn that way. Oh, dear, I don't like that dress at all, and doesn't she look lumpy in it!'"

Everyone but her mother laughed. "You would *not* be a maid," she said. "And it would be more respectable than showing off clothes and wearing lip rouge—and don't you dare tell me that you didn't, missy!"

"I'd choke if I had to wait on that spoiled brat all day long. Anyway, I'm going to see my friend at the theater today about the wardrobe job. That's more my style. And who knows where it will lead? And Kate will come, too, and we'll have a grand time and have sodas afterward at the drugstore to celebrate out new jobs."

But Kate was looking slowly from Ellen to Mrs. Flannery, thinking hard. She never wanted to return to office work, and perhaps working behind the scenes in a theater would not be so interesting after a while. If there were a chance to see Ireland, she could be the best maid—or companion—in the entire world.

She said, "Do you think Dr. Logan would consider me?"

"Oh, no," Aunt Grace said. "Your parents, God rest them, wouldn't have wanted you to be someone's maid."

"*Companion,*" Kate said firmly. "Mrs. Flannery, would they consider me?"

Mrs. Flannery studied her thoughtfully. "You're younger than Miss Logan. Mrs. Conner said the doctor wanted someone her age or perhaps a little older."

"I can look older!" Kate said. "I can! I will! And think of the money, Aunt Grace."

And Ireland, she thought. The vision of her mother's green fields almost blinded her.

Mrs. Flannery sighed. "I suppose it's worth the trying. It'll be a fine position with a good family. But I told Mrs. Conner that I'd be sending Ellen."

Ellen shook her head firmly. "I won't do it, Ma."

Mrs. Flannery hesitated for a moment, and then laughed. "Ah, why not. What's the worst thing that could happen? I'll telephone and tell Mrs. Conner that Kate is coming instead, because my daughter has other plans and they're so elegant that she can afford to pass up an opportunity like this."

Ellen laughed disrespectfully and sipped her tea.

Kate nearly collapsed against the back of her chair. "Do you think she'll like me well enough to ask the doctor to hire me?"

"Oh, she's doing the hiring," Mrs. Flannery said. "But why shouldn't she like you? If she asks how old you are, just look her straight in the eye and say, 'I've seen the death of my mother and my father, and my house fell flat around me and burst into flame.' By the time she sorts out all your tragedies, she'll forget about your age."

"Shame on you, Ma," Ellen said, yawning. "You're a bad example."

"Sure I am," her mother agreed. "It's that kind of a world sometimes." She bustled out of the kitchen, and the women heard her voice on the telephone in the hall, but they could not make out the words. Kate clenched her hands so hard that her nails bit into her palms, and from the corner of her eye she saw her aunt's disapproving expression. Forty dollars a month and a chance to see Ireland. She had never been impulsive before. But she knew that if this opportunity was lost to her, she would only find another office job and the years would pass, and she would never see the place where her mother was born, that Ireland so different from San Francisco, that cool green place . . .

"She'll see you," Mrs. Flannery said when she returned to the kitchen, smiling. "She asked that you come at three-thirty."

"But dearie, think this over," Aunt Grace cautioned. "Ask questions. You don't want to be just a maid."

"They're lovely people," Mrs. Flannery said. "Mrs. Conner wouldn't have stayed with them all these years if they hadn't been good folk."

But all Kate thought was *Ireland!*

Kate appeared on Dr. Logan's porch at exactly three-thirty and rapped the knocker firmly. But her mouth was so dry that she was not certain she could speak.

A small, stout woman dressed in black appeared in the door and lifted her eyebrows. "Are you Miss Keely?" she asked.

Kate nodded and said, "Yes, ma'am."

"I'm Mrs. Conner. Come in. We'll talk in the library."

Kate tried to smile, but her face was too stiff, so she concentrated on remaining very erect with her head high as she followed the housekeeper into a wide, dim hall. "Over here," Mrs. Conner said, leading the way into a small room filled with ceiling-high bookcases. "Please sit down."

Kate sat on an upholstered chair, opposite from the small sofa where Mrs. Conner settled herself.

"Dr. Logan wants someone who is between eighteen and twenty," the housekeeper said. "Don't lie to me and say that you are that old."

Kate blinked, shocked, and finally shook her head. "I won't lie," she said. But she did not tell her age. Instead, she said, "I'm very strong and I learn quickly."

"Where is your family?"

"My parents are dead," Kate said. "I've been living with my aunt."

"Do you have experience as a companion?"

"No," Kate admitted. "I worked as a clerk in the bookkeeping department of a hardware store."

"Do you have experience caring for a home?"

"Yes," Kate said, letting out her breath with relief. "My aunt and I live in Mrs. Flannery's boarding-house, and I help take care of the bedrooms and the rooms downstairs." Then she added, "I can't cook very well."

Mrs. Conner smiled. "Joseph cooks for us, and his nephew helps in the kitchen. We have two women who come in to clean the house twice a week, as well as a laundress, and a gardener who is also Dr. Logan's driver. I hope to hire at least one daily maid soon. Do you sew?"

"Yes," Kate said. "I made the dress I'm wearing."

Mrs. Conner seemed surprised. She leaned forward and studied the dress carefully. "You did this by yourself? No one helped you?"

"No one," Kate said proudly. "I have been making all my clothes for six months. I get the patterns from magazines and the cloth from stores in Chinatown."

Mrs. Conner tapped her chin. "Miss Logan has a dressmaker. But her clothes need care."

"I can do that," Kate said firmly.

"Mrs. Flannery probably told you that Miss Logan is ill."

"Yes, and I'm very sorry," Kate said. "I can do simple nursing. I took care of my aunt when we were refugees in Golden Gate Park."

"Miss Logan often needs physical assistance. She can't be left alone. A companion would have to help her dress and sometimes even support her. Perhaps even lift her."

"I can do that," Kate said.

Green hills unfolding and unfolding . . . Ireland might be ahead of her. Other people have adventures. Why not Katherine Keely?

Mrs. Conner regarded her soberly for a long moment. Kate could hear a clock ticking somewhere in the house.

Finally, Mrs. Conner said, "Dr. Logan trusts my judgment, so if his daughter likes you, we'll see how you work out—for a month. After that we'll discuss it again. Your salary will be forty dollars. You will have Sundays and Thursday evenings for yourself. No guests will be allowed in your room. You can wear your own clothes— a uniform would not . . ." She hesitated. "We do not think of this as a maid's position, although we need you to help with the bedrooms. We expect you to accompany Jolie whenever she leaves the house and make yourself available here to read to her or simply sit with her, if that's what she wants. Do you agree?"

"I agree!" Kate said and then realized that she had spoken too loudly. She caught a glimpse of Mrs. Conner's smile, gone almost before she saw it.

Mrs. Conner got to her feet. "We'll go up and meet her now."

Kate followed her up the carpeted stairs and waited while she rapped on a door and then opened it. "Jolie, I have someone for you to meet."

Kate stepped in and saw a pale, thin girl lying on a bed under a pink silk cover. Her blond hair was swept back in a loose knot, and she wore eyeglasses and a white quilted dressing gown embroidered with flowers. Gasping a little, she sat up when Kate came in, and her smile was cool and polite. She was watchful, and Kate's skin prickled under her scrutiny.

"This is Katherine Keely," Mrs. Conner said. "She'll help you for a month or so. Won't that red hair cheer us up?"

Jolie Logan studied Kate's face for a moment and the smile disappeared. "I know you from somewhere," she said slowly, thoughtfully.

Kate, surprised, said, "I don't remember seeing you . . ."

Jolie still stared, unblinking, at her. "I remember your hair. It's so very . . . *red*. It was tangled and dusty and hanging down your back. You were one of the refugees that passed this house, and you were with a family. With your mother and someone Mrs. Conner knows. I remember *exactly*."

"My mother is dead," Kate said. "But I did come down this street. I was with my aunt and our friends."

"Your mother is dead?" Jolie asked. She leaned forward, too intent now, and Kate nearly moved back a step.

"She died when I was six," Kate said.

Jolie leaned back on her pillow and turned her head to the window, as if she had lost all interest in the conversation. "All right," she said wearily.

Kate could not stop herself from asking, "Why should you remember me?"

"I remember every single thing that happened when my mother died," Jolie said. *"Everything."* She closed her eyes, clearly shutting Kate out of her thoughts.

"So do I," Kate said quietly. But anger boiled in her. *I don't believe I can work for her,* she thought. *She despises me. And I will end up despising her. But Ireland . . . If there's a chance . . .*

She followed Mrs. Conner out the door and was astonished to see the woman smiling. "She seems to like you well enough," Mrs. Conner said.

Kate kept her opinion to herself. She thought that Miss Jolie Logan was the most spoiled, rude, insufferable snob she had ever met.

As they walked downstairs, Kate said, "Mrs. Flannery mentioned that there might be travel . . ."

"That has yet to be decided," the woman said crisply. "It's probably unlikely. Come tomorrow around nine, with your belongings. I haven't decided which bedroom I'll give you yet, but you need to be available to Miss Logan during the night, so you won't be on the third floor."

The two stood by the front door, and Kate realized that Mrs. Conner had not asked her if she wanted the job after meeting Miss Logan. It was assumed that she would.

"I'll see you tomorrow, then," Mrs. Conner said as she opened the door. "Good-bye."

Kate found herself on the porch with the door closed behind her. She hesitated a moment, looked up at the tall trees that shaded the south side of the house, and wondered if Ellen had found work at the theater. Would it be better than this?

She walked slowly toward the streetcar. What have I let myself in for? she thought.

CHAPTER 6

Jolie

JOLIE HAD forgotten Kate the moment the girl was out of sight. She had spent most of the afternoon fretting over the new draperies at her mother's bedroom windows. They were not just the same as the old ones, and anyone who was not blind could see that! Father had promised that the entire house would be restored exactly the way it had been when Mother died, but Jolie could see that he was losing patience with her fussing about details that were so important to her and apparently only trivial to him.

"Your mother would not want this place turned into a shrine," he had said. She felt as if she had been slapped. A shrine? *Certainly not!* She only wanted the house to seem like her *mother's* home, quiet and serene and beautiful. Why was that so hard to understand?

The next morning she was back in her mother's room, plucking at the draperies again, when Kate stepped through the open door and said, "Mrs. Conner told me to let you know that I'm here. Can I do anything for you, Miss Logan?"

"Call me Jolie," Jolie said irritably, without looking up at the girl. "This was my mother's room, Katherine. Once it was the most beautiful bedroom I'd ever seen, but the people who made the new draperies used the wrong lining. It's so stiff and ugly! See how they poke out? They'll have to be done over."

She was having difficulty getting her breath, but she did not want this *companion* the housekeeper had hired to know how vulnerable she was, so she made her way to her mother's bed and sat down, careful to keep her spine erect and her hands folded quietly in her lap. "Which room did Mrs. Conner give you, Katherine, the one across from mine or the one next to the bathroom?"

"I'm called Kate," the girl said. "She gave me the room across the hall from yours, so I can hear you if you call." Kate turned slowly and looked around at the dainty French wallpaper, the delicately carved furniture, the pink flowered rugs, the heavy rose silk spread. "It's wonderful. How lucky that the mirrors didn't break."

"They *all* broke," Jolie said. For a quick moment, she remembered the sound of breaking glass and caught her breath. But then she composed herself and went on. "Every mirror in the house! But Father had them replaced. Most of the furniture was all right, and people came to repair the other things that were broken." She thought of asking this Kate person how *she* had fared, but obviously she had been left homeless, because Mrs. Conner had said that she was living in a boardinghouse.

"It's all lovely," Kate said. She moved toward the door. "If you don't need me for anything, I'll unpack now."

"I don't need you, thank you," Jolie said sharply, suddenly overwhelmed that Kate had not known her mother, who had decorated this room herself, and so the girl could not possibly understand the loss. She made a dismissive gesture that her mother would never have made. She did not look toward the doorway until she knew Kate was gone.

Hardy. That was what Mrs. Conner had called the girl, and she knew her father would agree. A hardy, strong, red-haired girl who could lift her when she fell, and help her in and out of bed on her bad days, and hook her into her clothes. A girl whose mother had died long ago, but who could manage without her. Probably she had always managed without her. But how? *How?*

Jolie could see her reflection in the pier glass. Her cheeks had flamed with that revealing blush she hated so much. How could I have been so rude to the girl? she thought miserably. *Why* do I do things like that? I would disappoint Mother so much. Oh, what of it, what of it? In a hundred years, who will know or care what I said to a maid on her first day in the house?

Jolie saw that her straight slippery hair was untidy, and she smoothed it back with her palms, but it would not stay up in a knot like her mother's. Kate had the kind of hair Jolie envied, rich and thick and coiled in place with only a few small tendrils curled around the temples. Oh, yes, she was hardy and healthy, and pretty in her own way. One look would tell you that she had never had a serious illness in her life.

Mrs. Conner stuck her head in the doorway. "Are you still in here, Jolie? Don't worry about those curtains. They'll hang out in good time. Come downstairs and have tea and look at the mail. Kate and I will be doing the bedrooms now."

Jolie got up, already weary by ten in the morning. "Was there anything in the mail for me?"

"Only the letter you've been waiting for," Mrs. Conner said, laughing.

Jolie's step lightened, and she hurried down the stairs. The tea tray had been set up in the library, and the mail was stacked next to it, all four letters for her. The one on top was addressed in a bold hand, and she tore the envelope open in such haste that it ripped almost in half. Never mind that. What does he say? Oh, yes! David Fairfield would be home from Los Angeles on Sunday afternoon! That was tomorrow!

She read the brief letter three times before she filled her cup, and then she read it again. It was so typical of the way David wrote to her, filled with slang and teasing, and she adored it.

"Hello there, Jolie," David had scrawled in his over-sized hand in bold black ink. "I hate this jay place—it's hot and dusty and the streets are filthy—so you'll be glad to hear that your boy will be on his way home Sunday if the train is still running. I'll toss you a surprise as I pass by. Love, your own Dave."

This was his private language, she was certain, saved just for her. He never spoke like that when he was at the house, especially around her father. *Never* around her father! David would be starting his medical studies soon, and Father would be one of his instructors at San Francisco University. In a few years, he would be Dr. David Fairfield.

Dr. and Mrs. David Fairfield, she whispered to herself. Mrs. David Fairfield. Father would let them have the house, of course. What use would he have for such a big place, when there were smart new apartment houses going up all over San Francisco? Mother would have been pleased with the marriage. She had always liked David and his family.

Jolie sorted through the other envelopes without much interest. An invitation from the Verts for their dinner party, a letter from Annie and Peter Prescott, who were traveling in Canada, and a thick letter from her aunt Elizabeth in Ireland. She would open them later, after she read David's letter again.

Joseph, their cook, came in with a plate of hot toast and the news that two women were waiting in the kitchen for Mrs. Conner.

Jolie raised her eyebrows. "Then please run upstairs and tell her."

Joseph fidgeted, his tiny brown hands clasping and unclasping. "Those women should not be left in my kitchen with only Nephew to stand guard."

"*What?*" Jolie got to her feet. "What do you mean?"

Joseph shrugged, scowled, and shrugged again. "They *say* they come from that downtown place that did *not* send Kate, but they are not supreme—or clean."

Jolie, puzzled for a moment, pushed her glasses up in place and frowned. Then, "Oh!" she exclaimed, suddenly enlightened. "You mean they're from the Supreme Domestic Employment Company?"

Joseph nodded, apparently relieved that Jolie remembered the name. Then he added, "They do not belong in *my* kitchen. Nephew is watching them so they do not touch the food."

Jolie sighed and started for the stairs. "All right. Go back to the kitchen and I'll get Mrs. Conner. Heavens! Now what?"

Staffing the house was difficult. The rebuilding of San Francisco offered more employment than had ever been available before, and people were pouring into the city. Domestic work was at the bottom of anyone's list of hopes. Mrs. Conner had made it clear that they were unbelievably lucky to get Kate at any price, and she had reminded Jolie rather firmly of the series of unsuccessful companion-maids that had preceded the red-haired girl. If the agency had sent two maids who worried Joseph so much that he was afraid to leave the kitchen, they undoubtedly would be unemployable.

She explained to Mrs. Conner as soon as she found her, and the housekeeper fled downstairs, muttering to herself. Kate, tucking in the blanket on Dr. Logan's bed, looked up at Jolie in surprise.

"Is there something I can help with downstairs?" she asked.

"Only if you're strong enough to throw people out of the house," Jolie said. "We've been trying to find maids . . ." She stopped, embarrassed. "Household help, people to do the hard things . . ." She stopped again.

Kate's dark green eyes were unblinking. "It's all right to say 'maid,'" she said stiffly. "I know what I am."

"You're *not* a maid," Jolie protested, embarrassed. "You're . . ."

Kate turned her back pointedly and smoothed the blanket under big strong hands. Jolie saw her own reflection in the mirror over her father's dresser. Her cheeks were practically *purple*.

"I'll leave you to your work," she said haughtily, and as she walked out of her father's room, she thought—for a moment—that she heard Kate's smothered laugh.

Drat that girl. *Damn* that girl!

Oh!

Jolie covered her mouth, even though she had not spoken aloud, and hurried down the stairs. She could hear Joseph shouting in Chinese in the kitchen, and a door slammed with a force that shook the house.

Mrs. Conner walked through the hall, patting her forehead. "Well, I never," she said vaguely. "And dirty fingernails, too!" She passed Jolie on the stairs, advised her to finish her tea, and continued on to the bedrooms. "Hussies," she said as she disappeared.

"Let Kate do the heavy work," Jolie said, but not loudly enough to be heard. Uncomfortable, somehow humiliated by the events of the last moments, she returned to her tea, now cold, and her letters. Once a month Aunt Elizabeth sent ten pages of complaints and exclamations of pleasure about her travels and her home in Ireland, most of which Jolie only skimmed. Aunt Elizabeth had married Charles Cross when she was in her thirties, had no children, and had involved herself enthusiastically with his efforts to help the Irish women in the village establish a small factory that produced fine embroidered linen. Jolie, who did not sew or embroider, had always been bored with the news of the factory but enchanted by her aunt's descriptions of the countryside and Europe. She skimmed the new letter, looking for the words *parties* and *gardens*.

But then one sentence caught her attention. "Charles will go to London to see a physician there."

She went back to the beginning of the paragraph and read about the man's health problems. Mother will feel so sorry about this, she thought. She knows Charles and likes him so much.

Jolie looked up from the letter and remembered, remembered, with more pain than she thought possible.

My mother is dead.

The morning seemed to darken. Outside, dimly, she heard the irritable toot-toot-toot of a boat in the bay and the rattle of a cable car.

She dropped the letter on the table and leaned back, overwhelmed. Sometimes she caught herself hurrying from one room to another, looking for her mother, eager to tell her something. Sometimes she even thought that she felt her mother's hand brush her arm. How did one survive this?

The house must be perfect again, Jolie thought fiercely. Perfect, in a remembrance of Mother—and for my own daughter one day, whose name will be Amy Knight Logan Fairfield. And she will wear a gray Worth dress to the opera.

Dr. Logan was coming home for a few minutes after lunch, which was unusual, but he had said that morning that he wanted to meet Kate. Jolie was still in the library when she heard the tinkling bell that Joseph rang for meals, but the dining room was empty when she reached it. As she took her place, she distinctly heard Kate, in the pantry, saying, "I can't sit in there. I just can't."

"You're supposed to," Mrs. Conner hissed. "Get in there and find something to talk about."

"Am I supposed to serve?" Kate whispered back.

"Of course you won't serve. You're a companion. Go in there and be . . . be companionable."

Kate seemed to be propelled through the swinging door, and Jolie, knowing that Mrs. Conner had pushed her, hid her smile by looking down at the tablecloth. Kate hesitated near the table and finally asked, "Where shall I sit?"

"Across from me," Jolie said, looking up. "Do you have something to talk about?"

"What?" Kate blurted. To Jolie's satisfaction, her face turned red.

"I heard Mrs. Conner telling you to be companionable. I only wondered how you planned on doing that."

Kate blinked. "I suppose I should talk about anything that interests you," she said after a moment.

Jolie's smiled tightly. Her earlier embarrassment at Kate's hands was fresh in her mind. "What did you think of *The House of Mirth*?"

Mrs. Conner had come in with the soup, and she looked sharply at Jolie, who ignored her smugly.

Kate unfolded her napkin. "I liked the book," she said calmly. "I'm looking forward to reading something else by Edith Wharton."

Jolie stared at Kate. "You enjoy reading?"

Kate looked up and smiled. "Oh, yes. When my father was alive, he brought books home all the time. People left them in the office and everyone passed them around."

Jolie lifted her spoon to her mouth, hesitated, and said, "What did your father do?"

Kate touched her mouth with her napkin. "He was a reporter for the *Call.*"

Mrs. Conner left the room, smiling in a way that caused Jolie to think that she was satisfied with the answer. Jolie was frankly surprised. An Irish girl whose father had been a reporter. Kate was no ordinary companion. "What happened to him?" she asked. Her voice was a little softer now.

Kate blinked again and finally said quietly, "He was killed in an accident on Market Street two years ago, when he tried to catch a runaway horse that a man had been beating. He loved horses. He got in the way of an auto, and it ran him down. It killed the horse, too."

Stunned, Jolie could think of nothing to say for a moment. Finally she said, "I'm terribly sorry. I'm really terribly sorry."

"Thank you," Kate said quietly. She went on with her soup.

Kate's loss cost Jolie her appetite. It had not occurred to her to ask questions of Mrs. Conner about the girl who would be moving in. She was just one more of a series of unsatisfactory maid-companions, poorly schooled and tiresome. But now Jolie wondered what her mother would have thought of all this. She had always expressed concern for the servants. She had always shown interest in their families.

"Then you've been living with your aunt?" Jolie asked, doing her best to sound the way her mother always had, gracious and interested.

"Yes, in a boardinghouse in the Western Addition. Our house was destroyed by the earthquake and the fire."

"And you went down this street with the other refugees," Jolie said. "I remember. It's like a photograph that I can't get out of my mind. All those poor people— and most of them never said a word. They just walked past in long lines, as far as I could see."

"We stayed in Golden Gate Park for weeks," Kate said. "We and the Flannerys, in two tents. After a while it seemed like an adventure. My aunt had been badly injured just before we reached the park, so she was in a hospital and we couldn't find her at first, or Mrs. Flannery's older boy, who had been conscripted to clear the streets. But in the end, we were all together again."

"I was in the park for two days," Jolie said. "Mrs. Conner and I. But I was ill, so our friends, the Prescotts, took me in their boat to Marin County, and I've been there ever since, until last month, that is. I'm recovered now, of course. My father wouldn't even let me come back for my mother's funeral, but I visit her grave every week. Do you visit the graves of your family?"

Kate nodded her thanks while Mrs. Conner removed her bowl and put down a plate with creamed potatoes and a small slice of ham. "No, not often." Jolie watched Kate hesitate for a long moment, without touching her food. "It never helped."

"I'm sorry," Jolie said quietly.

The silence in the room was so profound that Jolie wondered if Kate could hear her heart beat. She had gone too far with her companion, exchanging earthquake stories. And losses. But she was unsure of the boundaries between them. How much does one share? Where does she draw the line at confidences?

Dr. Logan bustled in then, smiling, exuding the scent of cigars and something medicinal. "Hello there, young ladies," he boomed. He bent to kiss his daughter and then said to Kate, "You must be Katherine Keely. I read your father's columns all the time. He certainly knew his California history. Do you know Peter and Annie Prescott? They often do pieces for the *Call.*"

"I met Mrs. Prescott once," Kate said. "In my father's office. And I'm called Kate."

"Well, we're glad to have you here, Kate," Dr. Logan said. He looked around, reached out for the cup of coffee Mrs. Conner held out to him, and said, "I can't stay long, ladies. I only wanted to look in on you." He took one sip of the coffee and handed it back to Mrs. Conner. "I'll see you this evening at dinner," he said. "And Jolie, now that Kate's here, consider getting out of the house and around town a little. What about having tea tomorrow afternoon at the Fairmont? You're well enough. You and Kate could join some of your friends. Mrs. Vert assured me that she and her daughter will be there."

Jolie withered in her chair. "I'll think about it, Father," she said. She had not gone out since her return from Marin County, and she was not prepared to see her friends away from the house yet. It was too big a step. And she had no idea how to behave in public with a companion. Her father had explained that she could not go about without one, but it was so awkward. But how did one explain a "companion"? Only ancient Mrs. Lee had one, a thin, worn creature who rarely spoke.

Kate did not look up from her lunch, and Jolie could not read her expression.

Jolie went to her room after lunch to rest, and as the afternoon progressed, she felt increasingly ill. Her heart fluttered at first, then pounded violently. When Kate looked in on her at four, to see if there was something she needed, she asked the girl to help her undress. "I won't go down for dinner," she said. "Please ask Joseph to send up something."

"Are you sure?" Kate asked. "Do you want Mrs. Conner to send for your father? If you're ill—"

"I'm *always* ill!" Jolie cried, exasperated into truthfulness. "Why do you think you're here?" The sight of Kate, so healthy, so robust, made everything worse. Why could not Mrs. Conner have found an old woman for a companion, one who was feeble and ill herself, someone to sit by the bed and read to her, not this great, strapping girl who had obviously never had a sick day in her entire red-haired, sassy life?

Kate flushed. "I'm sorry. Here, let me help you. Can you stand up while I unhook your dress?"

Jolie got up, wincing. Her knees must be swollen again. They hurt so much! Was there never an end to this rheumatic disease? This heart disease?

Kate patiently unfastened her belt and unhooked the dozen hooks that held the front of the silk bodice in place, then unhooked the bodice from the skirt. She hung it over the back of a chair and untied the skirt, which fell with a whisper to the floor. Jolie would have stepped out of it, but Kate said, "Wait. I'll do your petticoats at the same time." While Jolie waited, Kate untied both delicate linen petticoats and let them drop, then helped Jolie step out of them. Quickly, she whisked the pile of fabric away and began unhooking Jolie's corset. "Suck in your breath," Kate told her. "It'll be easier."

"Do you ever wish you didn't have to wear stays?" Jolie asked, gasping a little in relief when the garment had been tossed aside.

"Every day," Kate said, laughing a little. "I saw a drawing of a woman's bicycling costume in a magazine, and there were no stays in the bodice, and the article said that the women who have them do not wear corsets."

"What on earth do they wear, then?" Jolie asked, astonished.

Kate tossed Jolie's stays to the chair and looked around. "Where are your nightgowns?" she asked.

Jolie pointed to the chest of drawers next to the wardrobe. "Second drawer. What do the women wear, if not corsets?"

"Bands," Kate said, lifting a white nightgown out of the drawer. "They have bands they wrap around their . . . um . . . chests. Upper bodies, I mean."

"Well, I might be able to do that, but you certainly couldn't," Jolie observed. Kate had a more generous bust than Jolie.

"I know," Kate said. "The article didn't offer any solutions, and I could only imagine . . ." She held out the nightgown and looked away while Jolie removed her chemise. As soon as the gown settled around Jolie's legs, she bent and stripped off her bloomers and stockings. She did not want Kate's help with those garments.

"Think of it," Jolie said, straightening up. "No corset. What was the bicycling dress like?" She took a deep breath, delightedly aware of her physical freedom without her corset. If she had been alone, she would have stretched and arched her back like a cat. Instead, she sat on the bed again.

"It wasn't really a dress," Kate explained. She picked up Jolie's skirt and petticoats and shook out the wrinkles. "Instead of a skirt, there were very full trousers, gathered at the waist—"

"*Trousers?*" asked Jolie. "Are you sure?"

"Yes, the magazine had a pattern for them. There would be seams between one's limbs, of course."

"I'd like to see *that* pattern," Jolie said. She pulled the silk quilt over her legs and lay back against the heap of pillows. "Not that I would want such a garment, of course. That's really going too far."

"I wouldn't mind trying it," Kate said slowly as she folded the petticoats. "You know, inside the house where no one could see me, just to find out what it would be like."

"We have a sewing machine on the third floor," Jolie said, suddenly remembering it. "You can use it whenever you want."

"Do you want me to make you a bicycling costume?" Kate asked, grinning. Jolie saw mischief dancing in her eyes.

"Certainly not," Jolie answered. But she was smiling, too.

Kate ate dinner with Jolie in her room that evening. Dr. Logan came in to have dessert with the girls, but left again, saying that he had not had a chance to read the newspapers yet that day.

"I miss John Keely," he said as he walked toward the door. "I miss his viewpoint."

"So do I," Jolie heard Kate whisper.

The moment was painful, so Jolie filled the silence with a request. "I'd like it so much if you read to me for a while," she said. "I'm halfway through *The Jungle*. Would you mind picking up where I stopped?"

"Your father lets you read that?" Kate asked with obvious surprise.

"Have *you* read it?" Jolie demanded.

Kate laughed, reluctantly. "Well, yes. I read a chapter at a time, when my aunt was out."

"Then don't chide me for doing what you did," Jolie said with satisfaction.

This could work out, she told herself as she watched Mrs. Conner take the dinner dishes away.

But the next day proved that it might not work out, after all.

CHAPTER 7

Kate

JOLIE LOGAN was so ill! Nothing had prepared Kate for how badly the girl's health had been impaired. She was so thin that her elbows and knees were bony knobs, and her collarbones were skeletal. The shadows under her eyes were purple by the day's end, and her hands trembled.

Kate lay awake for hours that first night, afraid to sleep for fear Jolie would call her and she would not hear. Why had not Dr. Logan hired a nurse?

Kate did not fall asleep until dawn, and then Mrs. Conner woke her almost immediately afterward, it seemed.

"What time is it?" Kate mumbled, sitting up in the strange bed, bewildered for a moment at her surroundings.

"It's eight o'clock," Mrs. Conner said. "I let you sleep

in because I knew you must be tired. But Jolie is awake now, and you'll have to help her with her bath. She had a bad night."

"She didn't call me!" Kate protested. "I would have heard." She prayed that it was true. What if she had *not* heard Jolie's call! She would lose this job, too.

"She says she didn't sleep much, but she didn't need anything. Come along, now! Dress quickly, and run a warm tub for her. As soon as we get a full-time maid, she can help you, but right now you must do most of the work up here."

Mrs. Conner was heading for the door when Kate called her back, whispering urgently to her, "Why don't they have a real nurse for Jolie?"

"Jolie hates nurses. She had so many for so long that she won't allow one near her. The doctor is never far away, and I can handle most problems until he arrives. Stop worrying! You'll be good for her. I heard the two of you laughing together yesterday."

Kate dressed, braided her hair, and wound it around her head. She had not even time to splash water on her face, and she had to force down resentment. If someone had told her, she would have set the small alarm clock Aunt Grace had given her!

Jolie was sitting at her dressing table, her glasses on crooked, pulling a brush through her thin hair. She met Kate's gaze in the mirror and shrugged. "I won't be able to get in and out of the tub by myself today," she said. "Sorry."

"Don't be sorry," Kate said. "I'm here to help."

They managed the bath, with Kate looking away in order not to embarrass Jolie. Jolie chose a skirt and shirtwaist to wear, and they were no less complicated than the dress she had worn the day before. Kate struggled with hooks and tiny buttons, wondering if it had ever occurred to Jolie that she might have a wardrobe of beautiful loose morning gowns instead of struggling in and out of the complicated clothing that fashion imposed on women. It was none of her business, however, although she did suggest that Jolie wear her soft slippers downstairs to breakfast.

"No one will see," she said.

"Just as no one would see that seam separating one's limbs in a bicycling costume," Jolie added. Kate did not know if she was teasing or being sarcastic and was afraid to risk any kind of response.

They descended the stairs slowly, to find Dr. Logan waiting in the dining room, already finished with his breakfast. "What kept you ladies this morning?" he asked. His voice sounded jovial enough, but Kate detected steel in it and thought that he might not be such an indulgent father after all. Not in every way, at least.

"I'm sorry, Father," Jolie said quickly. "My bath took longer than I thought."

Dr. Logan's glance flicked over Kate and returned to his daughter's face. "Well, I like what you're wearing. And I like what Kate did with your hair, too." He stirred another spoonful of sugar into his cup and added, "If you plan to have tea with your friends, I should order a taxi for you."

Kate watched Jolie unfold her napkin and smooth it carefully in her lap. "I'm not well enough for that yet, Father," she said. "Perhaps another time soon."

Dr. Logan looked at her from under his heavy eyebrows. "You should start going out a little, Jolie," he said sharply. "You will grow stronger with exercise, not with hiding in the house."

"Next Sunday, perhaps, Father," Jolie said. "I'm sure I'll be ready then." She buttered toast with an innocence that Kate suspected immediately.

What is she up to? Kate wondered. But she was relieved, because she had no desire to go to tea with Jolie's friends that day. Eventually she must face the complicated social problems of being a companion, but not yet.

To Kate's relief, Dr. Logan left for church, after telling his daughter that he would see her at dinner. He was spending the afternoon on a friend's boat.

Jolie picked at her breakfast and finally pushed her plate away. Kate, who felt as if she had not had a good meal for weeks, was considering how she might get second helpings from the kitchen when Mrs. Conner came in and offered her more of everything. She took away Jolie's plate and brought a clean one, then heaped it with scrambled eggs and ham.

"Don't fuss over your food," she said. "You need to eat in order to get well. If you don't like this, then Joseph will fix you something else."

Jolie shook her head and stirred the eggs around with her fork, finally tasting a small bite. Mrs. Conner left with a sigh.

"Mrs. Flannery's daughter put a box of fudge in my trunk," Kate said suddenly. "It's the best I've ever tasted. Would you eat that if I brought it down?"

"Fudge isn't healthy food," Jolie said, but she smiled.

"I know it's not healthy," Kate said. "But it's good. Do you want it?"

Jolie laughed suddenly and Kate ran upstairs for the box. As far as she was concerned, food was food, and Jolie looked as if she were starving. What difference did it make what she ate, as long as she did?

They finished the box of fudge and the rest of the coffee before Nephew came in to clear the table. "You're a bad influence on me, Kate," Jolie said as the boy left.

"I know," Kate said. Jolie's voice had seemed to have an edge to it, but she decided to pretend that Jolie was being friendly. "You should meet my friend Ellen. She's an even worse influence."

Jolie was restless all morning, and after lunch, she began pacing back and forth in the front parlor, watching out the tall windows that looked over the street. At two, she demanded that Kate help her change clothes. She pulled a plaid silk dress out of her wardrobe, but no sooner was she hooked into it than she changed her mind. It was a good thing, too, Kate thought, because the bright plaid made her look even more ill.

She finally settled on an elaborate blue dress, a mass of tucks and ruffles. Her hair was too plain for the dress, so Kate did it over, this time copying a style that Ellen often wore, hair piled on top of her head in a mass of twisted rolls and tiny braids. Kate was perspiring by the time she finished, but Jolie was pleased with the result.

"Now we can sit on the porch and read," Jolie said. "Get a book and I'll bring mine. No, I can't bring the one I've been reading. I know! Go down to the library

and get *David Copperfield* for me, and something respectable for yourself. Something that my father would
approve of, and don't pretend you can't guess what that
would be. Go on!"

Kate, indignant at being ordered around so brusquely,
ran down to the library and found the book for Jolie and a
biography of Queen Elizabeth for herself. When Jolie
joined her on the porch, without glasses, she took *David
Copperfield* and settled herself in a wicker chair near the
front steps. Then she changed her mind and moved to the
porch swing. Then she changed her mind again, and
moved around to the side of the house where she sta-
tioned herself in a small arbor near a pepper tree.

"What's going on?" Kate asked abruptly. She
doubted that Jolie could see ten feet without her glasses,
and her constant fidgeting was causing her to have
breathing problems. "You're expecting someone to come
by, aren't you?" She had no idea what Jolie had planned
for her afternoon, but she suspected that it was something her father would not like—and surely Kate would
be blamed.

"None of your business," Jolie said pertly. "Go ask
Joseph to fix us tea, so we don't look like we're *hovering*
out here."

"We *are* hovering," Kate said. Like vultures, she
added to herself. "But I'll get the tea."

They had scarcely finished their first cups when the
reason for the vigil on the porch presented himself. An
automobile stopped in front, the horn honked several
times, and a young man who looked familiar bounded
across the yard.

"David!" Jolie said, blushing. "What a surprise!"

"Surprise, my left foot," David Fairfield said as he flung himself down on the bench next to Jolie. "I wrote and told you I was coming home today. Hello? Who's this? Don't I know you?"

The last was directed at Kate. "I'm Kate, Miss Grace Keely's niece," she said. "And you're Mr. Fairfield, who drove my aunt to the emergency hospital when she was hurt."

"Kate Keely, of course," David said, obviously pleased at remembering the encounter. "You jumped out in front of my auto and nearly got yourself killed." He turned to Jolie and said, "You should have seen her! They were among the refugees heading for the park, but I thought all the banshees in Ireland were after me. 'Take my aunt to the hospital!' she yelled. I didn't dare turn her down, so we rearranged three other injured people and a few boxes of crackers—"

"Sardines," Kate said. "The boxes were full of cans of sardines."

Jolie sat stiffly, eyebrows raised. "I have no idea what you are talking about."

"The poor woman was hurt," David said. "Something fell on her—"

"Part of a building," Kate said. She had seen Jolie's expression, and she was chilled. "We were trying to avoid a mob ahead of us that was fighting over water, and we wanted to get through a yard where the house had been badly damaged, and there was another aftershock, and a wall came down."

"How terrible," Jolie said politely. She obviously resented David's friendly interest in Kate.

Kate could see her job—and all faint hope for a future journey to Ireland—disappearing. "I'll ask Joseph to make more tea," she said, and she fled to the house. Behind her, she heard David say, "Well, little pal of mine, tell me what you've been doing since I saw you running around in the woods last month."

When the fresh tea was prepared, Kate carried it slowly back to the arbor, in time to hear Jolie cry, "Harvard! But I thought you were going to medical college here."

She put the tray down on the small wicker table and poured a cup for David, carefully not looking directly at him. But she might as well have been invisible, because Jolie and he were staring into each other's faces intently.

"Only if I wasn't accepted at Harvard, Jolie," he protested. "You were right there when your father and I discussed this. He thinks the three-year course there would be better, and then I can come in with him at the hospital. And then when mother sent me the telegram saying that I'd been accepted—"

"Three *years!*" Jolie said.

"I thought you'd be pleased," he said. He picked up a slice of pound cake and put it down again distractedly without taking a bite.

Kate took her cup and stepped out of the arbor, pretending great interest in the rose garden. She moved far enough away so that she could not hear them talking, and she did not return to the arbor until David Fairfield had left.

Jolie was in love with him. And from what Kate had seen in his face, his feelings for her might not be so deep. She was Dr. Logan's daughter, and a very sick young woman. He pitied her and babied her. And he was leaving her in September.

After the automobile had turned the corner, Kate went back to Jolie, who was sitting quietly with her hands folded in her lap. "Are you all right?" Kate asked.

"Of course I'm all right," Jolie said coldly. "Why wouldn't I be?"

"You're very pale," Kate said. "I think you should come in for a while and rest. I'll get you into a comfortable robe and read to you." Jolie's appearance frightened her. Dr. Logan, spending the day on someone's boat, could not be reached. Why had they not hired a nurse for Jolie, even if she did not want one?

She led Jolie firmly into the house, trying not to show her alarm. At the foot of the stairs, Jolie stopped and said, "I forgot that you have Sunday afternoons off! Don't you want to visit your family?"

"They won't expect me today," Jolie said truthfully. "I had made no plans. Let's go upstairs. Can you make it? Do you want me to call Mrs. Conner to help us?"

"I can make it myself," Jolie said. But halfway up the stairs she stopped and pressed her hand against her chest. Her face was the color of lead and her lips were as blue as if she had been drinking ink.

Kate grabbed her and half-dragged her the rest of the way to her room. She undressed Jolie while she was lying on the bed, stripping her down to her chemise and not caring what Jolie thought. She found a velvet robe in the wardrobe and eased Jolie into it, then covered her with her quilt.

"I'll pull the curtains," she said. "It's more peaceful. Then I'll read to you for a while."

"Not Dickens," Jolie said. "I can't bear hearing about all those starving children."

"My friend also sent along a book called *Love's Lost Song*," Kate said.

Jolie's lips twitched. She closed her eyes and said, "Your friend is a valuable source of food and entertainment. I've already read it, but I wouldn't mind hearing again about the always ravishing Miss Duchamps."

Kate burst out laughing, and she was rewarded with another smile. She hurried out of the room, but by the time she was back, Jolie had fallen asleep. Kate sat next to her, watching her, worrying. Finally she crept out of the room and found Mrs. Conner in her third-floor bedroom, resting in a soft chair with her hair down, wearing nothing but a cotton wrapper.

"I'm worried about Jolie," Kate said. "She's asleep now, but she had a difficult time when Mr. Fairfield was here and she was exhausted by the time he left."

"How bad is she?" Mrs. Conner asked, getting to her feet.

"I don't know," Kate admitted. "I don't know how bad she gets. I can't help but worry."

Mrs. Conner hurried down to Jolie's room and stood by the bed, listening to her breathing. Finally she moved back to the doorway and said, "She gets much worse than this. What was going on?"

Kate hesitated, then whispered, "She quarreled with Mr. Fairfield."

Mrs. Conner shook her head. "Let's go to your room. I'll explain."

In Kate's room, Mrs. Conner confirmed what Kate had feared. Jolie had loved the young man for years, but he would never marry her.

"And now he's going back east to medical school," Kate supplied.

Mrs. Conner sighed again. "I was afraid of that. But it's better than having to watch him marry someone else here," she said. "As he was sure to do it sooner or later. His family is rich. Every unmarried girl in town is after him. And Jolie is . . ." Mrs. Conner stopped.

"Jolie is what?" Kate asked.

"Surely you see."

"See what?"

"That she won't live a long life," Mrs. Conner said. "Everybody sees it but her father and her."

Jolie spent three days in bed. On the first day, her father brought another doctor to examine her, who advised rest and liquids. Jolie slept most of the time and refused everything but water. On the second day, Jolie pushed her tray with the bowl of bouillon off the bed and ordered Kate and Nephew out of the room. She pretended to be asleep every time Kate or Mrs. Conner looked in, and told her father that if she was forced to eat soup, she would vomit it up.

Kate overheard Dr. Logan discussing hiring a nurse with Mrs. Conner, who asked him to give Kate a chance. Without embarrassment, Kate stood outside the library door and heard the entire conversation. She might lose this job because Jolie was mooning and drooping over a boy and deliberately making herself more ill than she had been. If Kate was fired, she would not miss Jolie, who was too spoiled to be tolerated, but the pay was good and the work was simple enough. And in books, companions traveled with their employers. If there were any chance at all . . .

Kate was ashamed of her thoughts. Jolie was truly ill, and she wished her well again, even if she never went to Ireland but married David Fairfield and spent all her days in this house.

On the third day, Kate waited until Mrs. Conner left to shop, then persuaded Joseph to fry Jolie a thick slice of ham, a potato, and two eggs. She filled a bowl with cut fruit and put it on the tray while Joseph, muttering darkly to himself, worked at the stove. Nephew, polishing a copper pan, caught Kate's attention and grinned, then ducked his head.

Kate carried the tray upstairs and plopped it on the bed. "Here is a lunch fit for a miner, and your father will fire me if he finds out that I'm giving it to you. Eat it and I'll read the naughty part of the book to you all over again. Tomorrow I have the afternoon off, so I'll get more novels from my friend and ask her to make fudge for you, too. And I know a place where I can get big sugar cookies—everybody likes those. I'll get enough to fatten you up like a pig. Then on Sunday, we're going downtown to have tea with your friends."

Jolie stared at her haughtily. "I will not eat like a miner. I hate greasy ham and fried eggs. And I haven't eaten a sugar cookie since I was five years old."

"Wonderful," Kate said. She pulled Jolie up to a sitting position and doubled a pillow behind her. Then she picked up the novel and turned to page 103. "Marcello found her in the pantry and swept her into his arms, pressing her breasts . . ."

Jolie sputtered surprised laughter. "You said 'bosom' when you read that before. The book says 'bosom'!"

"I'm in the mood to say 'breasts' today. And 'legs,' too. And if you don't eat, I may say 'male organ' loud enough to get Nephew out of the kitchen, wondering if he's lost his somewhere."

"You're deliberately being disgusting!" Jolie scowled again. "Don't be smart with me, miss." But she was having trouble keeping from laughing.

"Marcello's—" bawled Kate.

Jolie shrieked and clapped her hands over her ears. "Stop it! Stop it right now."

"Eat," Kate said. She cut a piece of ham and poked it at Jolie's mouth. "Eat and save your reputation in this fine neighborhood. And if you're very good and clean your plate, I'll tell you what the chauffeur next door has been doing with the Verts' second parlor maid in the gazebo after dark."

"Tell me while I'm eating," Jolie said. "It is awful?"

"She doesn't think so," Kate said. "I've heard that she wears the kind of bloomers that are open at the—shall I say *crotch?*"

"Oh!" Jolie cried. "You're utterly revolting!"

"Do you want to hear the rest? Then eat!"

After that, they developed a sudden, close friendship, and it bothered Kate as much as their mutual animosity had bothered her before. Jolie seemed almost too obliging. She and Kate went to tea on Sunday afternoons with Jolie's friends, who became accustomed to Kate's presence, although they never warmed to her. Jolie would always ridicule them on the way home, telling Kate not to mind them, and promising her that before long she would be receiving invitations from them, too, to the parties that Jolie was still unwilling to attend.

She was right. Kate received her first personal invitation in late August, and she and Jolie went together to an evening card party at the home of Merry Johnson, the prettiest young lady in San Francisco that summer. Kate did not play cards, but she stood behind Jolie and watched her triumphantly lay down an ace over someone's king.

"Wonderful," her partner, a young man with freckles, exclaimed triumphantly.

"Good for you," David Fairchild said. He had been watching the game, too, a little awkwardly. Jolie had been very cool to him all evening.

Maybe she's over him, Kate thought. But on the ride home in the Logans' automobile, it was obvious that she was not. "Did you see him watching Merry?" Jolie asked. "Did you see how he looked at her?"

"He didn't look at her any differently from the way he looks at anyone else," Kate said firmly, although she had noticed the glances that the two young people had exchanged. "And what do you care? He's leaving for Boston tomorrow, and he won't be seeing her again."

At that, Jolie began crying. "Yes, and I'll never see him again, either."

"Until next summer," Kate said. "Stop crying or I'll get Joseph out of bed to fry you a slice of ham."

"What would I do without you?" Jolie said, wiping her eyes.

Kate gritted her teeth. Maybe develop some common sense, she thought.

Kate hoped that David would write to Jolie, but after the first happy letter, he did not write again, nor even respond to the Christmas note she sent him. But Jolie was growing stronger as the months went by, and Dr. Logan, impressed with Kate's service, gave her fifty dollars for Christmas, all of which she spent on her friends in the boardinghouse.

The Verts gave a large New Year's Eve party, and Kate was invited, too. Kate's presence at social gatherings disturbed Mrs. Vert, but it was well known in San Francisco society that winter that Kate Keely went everywhere with Jolie Logan, or Jolie Logan would not put in an appearance. Jane Vert, who was growing sassier every day, had announced to everyone that she planned on developing some sort of lingering disease so that she, too, could have a companion as amusing as Kate, since she hated and despised and loathed every one of her friends.

Kate discussed everything with her aunt and the Flannerys when she went to the boardinghouse on Thursday evenings and Sundays. They were as fascinated at the goings-on in the Logan house as they would have been with one of Ellen's novels. They agreed with Kate that Jolie had become too attached to Kate.

"My mother always said that friends can get too close and end up quarreling just so they have an excuse to get away from each other," Mrs. Flannery said. "You need to be careful, my girl. That's a good job."

"Familiarity breeds contempt," Aunt Grace said, as she had said a dozen times before, not minding that both Kate and Ellen groaned and laughed every time. "You'd better distance yourself from her."

"She was worried that you were after that David Fairfield, and now she's so relieved that you're not that she's trying to make you her best friend," Ellen observed over her chocolate cake. "But she'll get bored with you. They always do, those rich girls. They have a best friend today and another one next week and forget both their names the week after that. I see it all the time."

"I knew a doctor's daughter in Ireland when I was young," Mrs. Flannery said, resting on her elbows the way she always did when she was about to begin one of the stories that fascinated Kate so much. "This girl was the richest in our town, and in the nearest three villages, too. She had—and this is a true tale I'm telling—she had a dress for every day of the week, when most of us were lucky to have the one we were wearing and God save us if we didn't have a sister the same size at home, waiting for us to get back so she could have a turn wearing it."

"Ma, is that the truth?" Ellen demanded skeptically.

"It is the truth, and don't you be questioning me again, miss," Mrs. Flannery said calmly. "And this girl— her name was Mary Augustinia, but we called her Mogg behind her back—she kept that pointed nose of hers up in the air wherever she went, and when she passed us by, she pretended she couldn't see us." Almost as an afterthought, Mrs. Flannery added with a sigh, "I hated her so much that I had to confess it."

"Whatever happened to her?" Kate asked.

"My cousin wrote me that she married the richest man in the county and only had one baby before she was widowed. Doesn't it make your mouth water?"

They laughed then, even though Aunt Grace clucked and shook her head.

"Even one baby is too many for me," Ellen said. "I'm going to work and live my own life and have some kind of career." Ellen, who had found work in the theater wardrobe department, had left in a month, disillusioned, and gone back to work in the smart clothing store that had employed her before to model frocks. Both Kate and Ellen dreaded the day that Jolie would take Kate into the store, and they already had made elaborate plans to pretend they had never met.

Kate was always glad to spend time at the Flannerys', for she still considered the boardinghouse to be her home. Occasionally, with permission from Dr. Logan, she would spend the night and be back at the Logan house before eight Friday morning. Jolie was always distressed by Kate's absence, and she asked dozens of questions. What did Ellen say and do? What did they have for dinner? What was Hugh up to these days? What about Joe, the pest? It occurred to Kate that Jolie might envy her because of the Flannerys.

But she never asked to visit with Kate, and Kate was

not surprised. It was all well and good to be curious about how the ordinary folk lived, but quite another thing to become involved with them.

Spring came early, with delicious warm days in February, when the brown hills around San Francisco turned green. Jolie and Kate rode out into the country twice a week in a car that Dr. Logan hired for them, and sometimes they brought a friend or two of Jolie's. The girls had picnics and gathered wildflowers, and Kate thought that they were quite ridiculous, pretending to be anything but what they were—lazy and vain creatures waiting for potential husbands to select them.

She and Ellen expressed scorn for these trips over their desserts on Thursday evenings, for both of them saw few advantages in marriage for women. Ellen had made plans for them. One day they would have their own smart shop and sell clothes to the women they found so tiresome. "They have money," Ellen admitted. "We might as well find a way to get some of it away from them."

Ellen had finally realized the value in learning to sew. The dresses she modeled were too expensive for her to buy, even with the discount the store offered her. But she learned to copy them expertly, with Kate's help.

"If we just had the money," Ellen mourned once. "If we could only find a bag of nuggets under the floorboards or a box of gold pieces buried under the walnut tree. Hugh says that a man who works in the morgue told him that maybe as many as four thousand people died in the quake and the fire—no matter what the

newspapers say—and that many of them were inciner-
ated, so they weren't found. So that means any money
they had on them is out there in the ash heaps, melted
into blobs. Someday people are going to start looking."

"Not us!" Kate exclaimed. "I don't care how many
'blobs' there are! Dead people's money! That's awful!"

Other times, Kate would say, "We must save. And
we need to find out things—how much it would cost
to rent a store, and how much it would cost to stock it
with what we want to sell. It's a very big responsibil-
ity." But in her heart, she could not imagine herself
being part of such a business. The more time passed,
the more convinced she was that she should live in Ireland, away from memories of falling bricks and
screaming people trapped inside buildings and the terrible gray dust drifting down. She needed and wanted
to be away from the unending racket and dirt of con-
struction—and the suffering horses that still died of
overwork, laboring to rebuild San Francisco. The small
amount of money she saved might someday accumu-
late and pay her fare, if her hopes about Jolie's traveling
never came to pass.

But Ellen's mood could change instantly, and she
would sigh and sink into a depression. "Who would buy
clothes from two San Francisco Irish brats?" she would
mourn at those times.

"Irish brats with money," Kate would console her.
"Everybody's working. Everybody needs clothes. You
could do it."

They would plan until Mrs. Flannery would finally
send them to bed, complaining that they were keeping

the boarders awake. Kate would fret guiltily, knowing that the plans for the shop were only second-best for her. She wanted to see the unfolding fields and the sea so far. She could find work in Ireland. No matter what anyone said about the impossibility of finding work there, she knew that she could, even if it was only as a maid somewhere. And she would experience all that her mother had experienced, growing up in that green and misty land.

She was fascinated with the stories Mrs. Flannery and Mary Clare told about Ireland, and she would beg for more until they would laugh and tell her that Ireland meant rain and frostbite and hard times, not just big families and old ladies who put out saucers of milk for the fairies at night. Both women had left the place willingly, and so they could not be expected to encourage Kate in her daydreams. She carefully avoided dwelling on her mother's willing departure. Once, when Aunt Grace had commented on Kate's mother's joy in San Francisco weather, Kate had excused herself from the table, in order not to hear.

In March, Dr. Logan received a letter from his sister-in-law in Ireland, saying that her husband had died and asking that Jolie come to spend time with her. "She is my only living relative," he read from the letter after dinner that night. "Jolie must come and see what will belong to her one day."

Dr. Logan put the letter beside his place and said, "It's obvious that she's made you her heir, Jolie."

Jolie, transfixed, sat holding her fork in midair. "Her

heir?" she asked. Kate could see that she liked the idea. "What's it like?"

Kate was in shock. Ireland, she thought. But it can't be this easy.

Dr. Logan shrugged and said, "I can't say that I've ever paid much attention to the descriptions of the house. I know that it's very large. And the estate is large, too. And there's that factory that makes bedding or something like that." He did not look directly at his daughter, and Kate held her breath, hoping he would find a way to manipulate her into going.

"Fine linens," Jolie said absentmindedly. "Embroidered linens with lace. I wonder what the people around there do with their time."

Kate stifled laughter. What did the people do? What people anywhere else did!

"Elizabeth spends time in London, doesn't she?" Dr. Logan asked, his eyebrows lifted in surprise. "Doesn't she go on and on about it? And Paris, too. I don't think she spends so much time on the estate."

"But still . . ." Jolie mused. "When she's not traveling, she's stuck there in the middle of nowhere. Dublin. Who goes to Dublin?"

"It has theaters and museums, and a big university," Kate supplied. She could not hide her smile.

Dr. Logan looked at her, startled. Then he obviously recognized an ally, because he said smoothly, "Kate is absolutely right. It's a cultural center, and it's not far from the estate."

Jolie tapped her fork against her place twice, three times. "Hmm," she said. "I don't like it. I've heard that the weather is awful. I'm sure Aunt Elizabeth will live for a long time, and I don't have to worry about anything for years."

"Jolie!" her father said. "She is making you her heir. You are her only living relative, and she's asked to see you. The least you can do is consider it. The travel will be wonderful for you. Getting away from this house will strengthen you."

"I don't want to leave my mother's house," Jolie said, and she got up and ran out of the dining room.

Dr. Logan sighed. "Well, I thought for a moment that she would consider it."

"Sorry," Kate said. Her heart had just broken. Jolie could not be made to go. As much as Dr. Logan wanted her to spend time with her aunt, now that her mother was dead, he could not force her. She would only get sick again from the pressure.

Dr. Logan drank the last of his coffee in one big gulp and then said, "You have a great deal of influence over her, Kate. Travel would be the best thing for her, now that she's enjoying improved health. I must be truthful with you. It's not likely that Jolie will ever marry. Certainly she could never bear a child—her heart is much too weak. If she interested herself in travel, the way so many women do, then her life would have focus. I've know women who spent years dawdling around Europe, in England and Italy and France. Ireland would be a start for her. She has family there, so she would have someone to travel with. Someone to look out for her."

Kate nodded dumbly. What was she supposed to say? Jolie would travel with her Aunt Elizabeth, and there would be no need for Kate, who knew nothing about travel in Europe anyway.

"See what you can do," Dr. Logan went on. "The trip could be managed, now that she's better. And the Prescotts are leaving for London in May. The two of you could travel with them all the way to Ireland."

The two of you. Kate was not sure she had heard him. She felt the blood rush to her face.

"You mean that you want me to go with her?" she asked.

"Of course," he said, looking at her strangely. "I couldn't let her go alone. You know how to take care of her when she's not too ill. Before you leave, I'll train you to care for her when she's having difficulties. And there are doctors aboard ship and doctors in Dublin. As far as traveling to the continent . . . it's an enticement, isn't it? Something for her to look forward to. I could join her two or three times a year—she can come home for short visits. There's always someone traveling back to California. Her life would be full. She wouldn't miss . . ."

Ireland! Kate thought, scarcely listening to him.

"I'll bring you to the hospital with me a few times, Kate," he mused, looking at the letter again. "You'll learn everything you need to know for the trip, I'm sure." He looked up at her sharply then. "But first, she must be persuaded. If everything goes as I hope, she'll come home in a few months feeling stronger, only to want to leave again as soon as she can, the way the Prescotts do. Her life will be exciting, even though she can't live it as a woman should."

As a woman should. Marry and have children. No,

Jolie could never do that. And Kate did not want to do it, either.

"I'll persuade her," Kate said, hoping that she really could.

"I thought you would," Dr. Logan said and he nodded once, briskly. She saw in his face that he knew what she wanted from this trip—passage to Ireland. "When you *bring her back* from her *first* trip in six months, you'll find a bank account set up for you that will guarantee your future. You'll be under no further obligation. And Jolie need know nothing of this. By that time, she should have developed a taste for travel—with your help. She'll have made friends among world travelers. With enough care, her health should steadily improve over the months. A new world will welcome her. And your future will be assured."

So that was it, the carrot to lead the donkey. Kate would not be abandoning Jolie in Ireland, not if she wanted the money enough. Dr. Logan was very clever.

If worst came to worst, there was Ellen's idea of a shop. Would there be enough money for that?

But no, no. It wouldn't come to that. Ireland. She would find a way to stay.

"Thank you," she said, doing her best to sound sincere.

CHAPTER 8

Jolie

ONE DAY no one knew about the proposed trip to Ireland, and the next day it seemed to Jolie that all her friends were aware of it—as well as the delightful news that she would one day inherit an estate there. The attention was thrilling, and she was *certain* that Merry Johnson was finally jealous of *her*. Even David, far away in Boston, wrote to demand that she give him all the details of her trip—and her inheritance. Jolie wondered, briefly, which of the two bits of news had made her interesting to him again, but she pushed the thought away and answered him enthusiastically. The trip was planned for May, she told him. Perhaps he could meet them in New York while they were waiting for the ship that would take them to Ireland.

Annie Prescott took Jolie and Kate shopping for traveling clothes, turning Jolie away from the delicate, crushable linens she preferred to sturdier fabrics in dark colors. Kate, oddly silent, accepted the clothes as a gift from Dr. Logan, along with luggage almost as nice as Jolie's. She seemed preoccupied each time she returned from the hospital where Father was putting her through some hasty—and unnecessary—training. But when Jolie questioned her about her willingness to go, she admitted that she had always wanted to see Ireland.

"But you won't leave me there," Jolie said instantly, seeing Kate's puzzling expression, excitement apparently mixed with regret. "The Prescotts will be staying in England. You wouldn't leave me in Ireland with strangers."

"Of course not," Kate had said briskly. "I'm an American, and San Francisco is my home, but I'll stay in Ireland as long as you do."

This answer was satisfying, Jolie told herself. Kate had promised, even though she was thoroughly a young woman of San Francisco and would never be content anywhere else. But anyone would be excited about the trip, although Kate missed two fittings because Father had dragged her off to the hospital to learn boring things from the senior nurse, and she was absent several afternoons after that, going on calls with him. Finally he gave Kate a neat leather case filled with bottles and boxes. Jolie, poking through it curiously, asked Kate what everything was for and received longer answers than she wanted.

"We won't need any of it," she told Kate. "I'm well now, and I won't get sick again."

There was barely time to stop to think before Mrs. Conner and the new upstairs maid, Agnes, began packing the trunks and small bags. Jolie, carried on a rushing tide of enthusiasm, ate better than she had and even gained a few pounds, which pleased her father. She kept silent about the occasional night attacks of pain and breathlessness. Everyone must continue to see her as well and happy—and fortunate. Merry Johnson, who had always been so pitying when Jolie was ill, must be greeted enthusiastically half the time when she called— and then told by Mrs. Conner regretfully the other times that "Miss Logan is not in," even though "Miss Logan" could be heard laughing upstairs with her companion.

It was all wonderful and exciting, and only on the last day did Jolie remember that she was leaving her mother's house, the quiet and beautiful refuge created by the quiet and beautiful woman who had raised her. She sat for an hour on the edge of her mother's bed, looking around, holding the gray Worth dress on her lap. Perhaps she would never be the wife of Dr. David Fairfield, although that could not be said for certain yet, but one day she would live here with a husband, and a daughter who would be named Amy, and everything would be perfect again.

The day of departure opened with thick fog, and even though they left for the ferry in plenty of time, the terrible morning traffic on Market Street delayed them. At last they reached the ferry building and met the waiting Prescotts. Dr. Logan had to leave in haste because one of his patients was in labor, so Jolie was turned over to the Prescotts for safekeeping. Several of Jolie's friends were there—but not Merry Johnson—and she was sorry for that. She would have liked watching Merry trying to smile. Kate's friend Mrs. Flannery was there, with Ellen and her tall and gawky brother, Hugh, and Jolie witnessed a charming moment when Mrs. Flannery blessed Kate's trip by drawing a cross on her forehead, saying, "Dearest girl, may the road always rise up before you and the wind always be at your back." Kate shed tears and hugged each of them, and Jolie realized that Kate had a true family, even though most of her relatives were dead.

Jolie took one long look at the fog that enveloped the city, cutting off any hope for a last view, and sighed before she turned to walk onto the ferry. "We're on our way, Kate," she said.

Kate hugged each of the Flannerys and hurried after her. Her cheeks were pink, her eyes bright. She's glad to be going, Jolie thought with satisfaction. And I won't be nervous or afraid. Good, sturdy Kate, almost as close as a sister now, would always be there.

But six months was such a long time to be gone! Six months away from her mother's house. Now, at this last moment, she could not believe that she had agreed to it.

The ferry, its foghorn moaning, plunged though the choppy gray water to Oakland, and there was a great rush of people at the dock, pushing in all directions without regard to anyone else's feet or elbows. Jolie hoped that Peter and Annie Prescott were able to keep track of the trunks and suitcases, for she was so overwhelmed by the noise and confusion that her knees were ready to give way.

At the train, she turned gratefully to Peter Prescott, who was holding out his long arm to her. Kate stayed behind with Annie, whose curly hair was coming loose from under her hat, to help with counting trunks and checking them off a list as porters carried them away.

"You look worried," Peter said to Jolie. He bent over her comfortingly. "Come on, child, smile. This is a great adventure for you. You'll love traveling, I know you will. Annie and I wouldn't do it if it wasn't wonderful."

But her heart was pounding and she was suddenly frightened. She bit her lip and hurried beside him, clutching his arm. Six months wasn't so long. And probably she would see London and Paris, too. Wouldn't her friends envy her for that! She would go to the places that her mother had visited on her honeymoon, and when she came home again, she would put her travel diary next to her mother's on her mother's bedroom bookshelf and feel that something important had been completed.

The Prescotts bundled her into the nearby train quickly. The ferry had been late, and even though it was not yet time for the train to leave, they were anxious to check on their accommodations. Jolie, Kate, and Annie would share a bedroom compartment, and Peter would have a berth right outside the door. The arrangements were important to Jolie, who did not want to be left alone, ever, and she suspected that those exact arrangements had been important to her father, too. Never mind that three women in one room would be crowded. Father wanted people watching over her.

The porter showed them the compartment and hung up their coats. Peter fussed around, rearranging cushions, adjusting the kerosene lamps, peering out of the window, and checking his pocket watch. Annie explained that when the beds were made up, Jolie would have the bottom bunk, Kate the upper, and she would take the small cot that folded out of a chair. Another porter brought in the single trunk the women would share for the journey to New York, while everything else would be put in the baggage car. "And probably lost," Annie said philosophically, smiling when the porters were gone.

"But you said it didn't matter," said Kate, who did not look convinced. "You said that it will be easy to replace things."

"Of course," Jolie said, answering for Annie. "We can buy whatever we need." She wanted to sound as if she were an experienced traveler, but she had grave doubts about the single trunk. Yes, they would have more room in the small compartment. But it was a long trip, with several train changes along the way in towns that she had never heard of until Father and Peter had shown her the itinerary and maps.

Other people do it all the time, Jolie told herself as she straightened her traveling skirt, sat down, and removed her hat. And Merry Johnson must be pulling out her hair by now.

After what seemed like an hour, the train started with a jerk, and Jolie watched the passing clutter of dirty old buildings outside, the nameless strangers, and the streets of Oakland. Kate sat next to her, head back and eyes closed, and Jolie wondered what she was thinking. Was she lonely for San Francisco already?

Kate, as if knowing that Jolie was looking at her, said, "We're going to have a wonderful time."

"Of course we are," Annie said firmly. Since the train was under way, she said she would leave them for a while and sit with Peter, and the girls would have room to stretch out if they were tired. But Kate made herself comfortable sitting by the window and opened her book, so Jolie tried to read, too. The train swayed from side to side, and the noise was maddening. There would be days of this, and they could not be certain just how many, the Prescotts had warned, because connections might be missed, and there might be washouts along the way. There often were, in May.

The four went to lunch in the dining car, but Jolie was unable to eat. She caught the look that Kate and Annie exchanged and told them that she preferred to have tea and toast in their compartment. The simple request required a great deal of embarrassing fuss, and Jolie finally asked Peter to take her back to the compartment, leaving Kate and Annie to struggle with arrangements for a tray.

"Every railroad is different, and some are more exasperating than others," Annie explained when the women were back together in the compartment. The tea had arrived cold, and the single piece of toast so dry that Kate had begun laughing when she saw it.

Peter had disappeared, intending to speak to the conductor, he had said. When Annie decided that Jolie would be better off lying on her bed, no one came to make it up. Jolie could not drink the tea and spent the afternoon dozing, sitting upright. When she woke, her neck was stiff, and she could not remember being more uncomfortable.

"Look at all the windmills we're passing," Kate said. Jolie saw dozens of them turning, turning, in a flat valley floor where small farmhouses had been scattered. Some of the houses even had windmills on their roofs.

"I've never been so far from home," Kate mused.

"You'll be going a lot farther than this," Jolie said. "Are you sorry you came?"

Kate's smile was her answer.

The trip became a nightmare for Jolie after that. The valley gave way to mountains, but a surprising snow-storm delayed them for hours in a small station. The car was freezing, and it reeked of coal smoke. The dining car produced only cold food, and the evening dragged on miserably. Somewhere a child cried monotonously.

Finally, when Jolie was numb with misery, the train started up again. Hours later they plunged down into desert territory, where the car filled with alkali dust. Jolie never left the compartment again. The dust made it difficult for her to breathe, and lying down was im-possible, so she sat up in bed and watched the ugly land-scape pass, wondering why anyone would live in such a terrible part of the country and why she was attempting to cross it.

Kate and Peter performed some sort of magic (prob-ably involving a great deal of money), and Jolie's meals were served on a tray by a sullen, uniformed woman. Kate read to her, and when Jolie could no longer keep track of the story, she would ask Kate to tell her about the Flannerys, how Hugh had become lost to them during the terrible time of the earthquake and was not found for a week, and how Mrs. Flannery was given money by her drunken cousin to start the boarding-house, and how Aunt Grace had taken the last of their insurance money to add to the down payment, and what the kind Italian banker had said to them when they went to him for a loan.

"All I did was stay in a cabin in the woods," Jolie said, not adding that the cabin had seventeen rooms and a full staff of servants.

The ugly flat plains were dotted with sagebrush, and the ground was white with alkali. Occasionally they saw houses but never people except at the small stations where the train stopped to load and unload people and freight. Their food was gritty with sand and their faces never quite clean.

"I want a bath," Jolie said once, desperately. "I can't stand this."

"You won't get a bath until we reach New York," Kate said sadly.

But she would, for they missed their connecting train in Ogden. They were ten hours late because of the delay in the snow, and they spent a night in a small, cramped hotel where the beds smelled sour. There was a bathroom on their floor, however, so for the outrageous sum of five dollars, a frowsy overweight woman promised to fill the tub halfway with hot water "that the bunch of you can share."

Jolie laughed weakly. "I'll give her another fifteen dollars," she said. "We can all bathe."

"That won't work," Peter said, his lips tight. "Heating that much water would take three more stoves and ten more women." Kate barked a laugh, but Annie, the experienced traveler, looked as if she would cry any moment.

At Jolie's insistence, Kate filled three basins with hot water for the others, and then Jolie undressed and stepped into the tub. No bath had ever felt better, even though the water was tepid by then. But when it came time to get out of the tub, she could not get to her feet and had to call weakly for Kate, who did not hear her at first. A man began pounding on the bathroom door, which was halfway down the hall from her room, and Jolie shrieked at him to get away. Kate's strong shout sent the intruder away, but Jolie was in tears when Kate reached her.

"I hate all this," she said as Kate wrapped her in one of the hotel's thin, rough towels.

"Thank God it can't get any worse," Kate said firmly.

But it did. Because they had missed the train, they did not have a compartment secured on the one that left the next morning, and the best Peter could manage for them were seats in the overcrowded coach filled with ragged elderly people, weeping children, and their frantic parents.

"Look on this as an opportunity to learn," Peter said when he had them settled in their seats.

"Peter!" shouted Annie, who was pushing away a small dirty boy who had casually climbed into her lap. "This is not an opportunity, it is hell."

"Blasphemy!" a dark-haired woman said. She had a

mustache and musty black clothing, and she carried a Bible in her lap.

Annie rolled her eyes. Jolie, too shocked to laugh, decided to store the moment in her memory for a time when she and Kate could discuss it and laugh about it. The train clanked and rattled toward Denver.

"If this doesn't kill me, nothing will," Jolie observed.

"Wait until we reach New York," Kate said. "Everything will be better." Her face looked pinched and her color was bad. She had begun coughing earlier in the day.

"You're ill, aren't you?" Jolie asked.

Kate shook her head, but it was obvious that she had caught a cold. Annie, listening from the seat ahead of them, reached back to touch Kate's forehead and announced that she had a fever.

"You have to do something, Peter," she said. "We can't stay on this car."

"Should I commandeer the train?" he asked. "Throw everyone off? Believe me, I've tried everything, including bribery and threats."

"That's a start," Annie said with a sudden laugh. Kate managed a weak smile.

The woman with the mustache had five children in the car, none of whom appeared to have a seat of his own, and the trip was made even less bearable by them. One of them busied himself by removing the screws that held his mother's seat in place, and when he had achieved the result he desired and her hard seat pulled loose, he tossed the screws into the crowd and laughed. She reached out a swift arm and caught him a blow hard enough to bloody his nose, and the boy retreated to the men's lavatory at the end of the car, where he bellowed for half an hour. A kind old man put the seat back together and peace fell on the car.

"And I thought the Flannery boys were awful," Kate murmured weakly.

Jolie looked at her and saw that tears were running down her face. "Don't you dare get any sicker," she said.

"I'll be fine," Kate groaned, and she coughed again. She dug through the leather case, found a bottle containing a thick, black syrup, and poured a dose into the small glass Dr. Logan had included. Jolie gagged sympathetically when Kate gagged.

"If that doesn't poison me, I'll be well tomorrow," Kate said as she wiped her mouth with a handkerchief. "What a terrible taste!"

That train had no dining car, so everyone who wanted to eat had to get off when it stopped briefly, bolt down the food purchased at small shops and stalls, and hurry back. Once, Peter and Annie got off long enough to buy a full meal for all of them in a restaurant near the station. They barely made it back, and while they worked their way down the crowded aisle, the children begged them to share. Their mothers had been feeding them nothing but the bread and sausage that they bought from the vendors who had hurried through the cars at some of the stops.

But Peter and Annie held their parcels above the reaching hands until they got to their seats.

"You bought china, too?" Jolie exclaimed.

"We even bought the tablecloth," Annie said, and

she shook it loose over the girls' laps. "Chicken and dumplings, and apple pie, and we even have a jug of coffee."

Jolie forced herself to eat, even though she was not hungry. Kate picked at the food, and left most of her portion for Peter. By the time the meal was over, she had fallen asleep, leaning against Jolie's shoulder. Jolie did not move. Night fell, and the train rolled noisily onward through wheat fields silvered by moonlight.

The next change of trains left them better off. The women were back in a compartment, although this one did not have its own lavatory. On the train after that, Peter paid the couple who had the only compartment twice its value and once again the women were comfortable. But the trunk that had contained their clothing had disappeared during one of the train changes. Rich or poor, passengers were responsible for their own belongings, and if one could not find one's trunk in the pile on the platform, the next train would not wait. Days and nights blended together. Mountains rose ahead and fell behind them, and between them, Jolie looked out at what seemed to be unending plains or forests. It was always cold in the mountains and hot on the plains.

"I'm going home by ship," Jolie announced when they finally reached New York. "I'm not going to Ireland and I'm not ever getting into a train again, not as long as I live. Eight days! It felt like eight months."

They were in a carriage, on their way to their hotel, when she said this, and Annie's laughter offended her.

"You think this was bad?" Annie asked. "Wait until you sail from New York to San Francisco. We've done it twice, but never again. The last time we spent two weeks sailing two miles against a storm off the tip of South America, with Peter sick every inch of the way."

Jolie leaned her head back and looked out at twilight on New York's crowded streets. The whole thing was hopeless. She had no sense of adventure, or whatever it took to make a traveler out of someone who had never wanted to leave home anyway. Beside her, Kate coughed, excused herself, and coughed again.

"Oh, go ahead and cough, Kate!" Jolie cried impatiently. "If there's anything I can't stand, it's a polite sick person."

"Stop talking," Kate croaked. "If you don't do another thing in this lifetime, stop talking."

Jolie was furious, but she knew that Kate did not care. Wretched maid, and that's all she was. A maid. And she had been coddled and fussed over for half a continent.

"I already hate Ireland," Jolie said to no one in particular.

Their room overlooked the street, where people came and went all through the evening. Peter had planned that they meet in the dining room for dinner, but Kate was too sick for that and Jolie was too tired, so the Prescotts went to dinner alone. Kate snored in bed, to Jolie's disgust, so she rang for a hotel maid and explained that she needed help with her bath. Silent and efficient, the woman helped Jolie out of her travel-stained clothing and stiff corset and held out a firm arm for her while she stepped into a blissfully hot tub. She promised to have the clothes back by morning, clean and pressed, but Jolie did not care if she burned them or threw them into the alley. She was sick of them. She sank back into the water and smiled. Lovely clean hot water.

Kate appeared in the doorway, coughing and red with anger. "What are you doing?" she cried. "Why didn't you wake me?"

"What?" Jolie asked, up to her chin in water and suds and in no mood to be scolded. "And stop your snuffling and snoring?"

"Oh!" Kate said, and she walked away.

The maid came back and helped Jolie out of the tub and into the nightgown that Annie had found in one of the trunks that had been delivered to their room. When the maid asked Kate if she wanted help with her bath, Kate shouted, "No!" The maid left without comment.

"It's your turn now," Jolie said when she walked into the room, rubbing her hair dry. Kate was lying flat on her back again. "I think you might feel better if you bathed," Jolie told her. "Your head wouldn't be so congested."

"I'd feel better if I died," Kate said, dosing herself with more of the black syrup.

"Don't die, please, until after someone brings up our dinner," Jolie said coldly. "It would look so tacky."

Kate got up wearily and began stripping off her clothes as she walked toward the bathroom. "Do I have a nightgown?" she asked. "Or are all my clothes lying in a field somewhere?"

"You have one of Annie's nightgowns, hanging on

the hook inside the door," Jolie said, feeling infinitely superior. "I wish the trunk we were sharing hadn't disappeared, but everything else we brought is here. We'll go shopping tomorrow and replace—"

Kate slammed the door and locked it.

Their ocean journey began two days later. David Fairfield had not come to New York, and Jolie understood, finally, painfully, that she was less interesting than his studies. By the time they left, Kate was almost well again, to Jolie's relief; their missing clothing had been replaced; and the girls had bought half a dozen paperbacked romance novels from a news vendor in the railroad station at the end of the block.

Jolie slept poorly at night. Her joints were painful, and sometimes, when she stood up too quickly, she felt dizzy. But she hid this from Kate and the Prescotts. The thought of returning to her father so soon after the terrible trip east kept her silent. She would be fine, the time would pass, and by some miracle, she would return home to San Francisco in the most boring—and comfortable—fashion possible. She had nothing to worry about, she told herself over and over.

Their cabin adjoined the Prescotts on the second-class section of a respectable, aging passenger liner. It lacked the luxury of some of the new liners, but their cabin was larger than they had expected, and it was close to the dining room and the lounge. They left New York on a perfect May morning, on a sea as smooth as satin, lunched happily with the Prescotts at a large table with half a dozen other people, and spent the afternoon in deck chairs, reading novels that their families would have forbidden.

"As soon as you stop coughing and sniffling, I'd like you to read aloud to me again," Jolie said. She enjoyed Kate's way of reading, and she was more tired than she wanted to admit. Sometimes her heart seemed to struggle too much, and her knees were swollen, always a bad sign.

"Oh, I'd be happy to read to you now," Kate said. She eyed Jolie's book and read aloud the title. "*The Island of Lost Love,* by Mrs. Esmerelda Damone. Why are all of these authors married women, do you suppose?"

She had attracted the attention of two elderly women sitting next to them, just as she had intended, Jolie suspected. Jolie said, "Because only married women know the secrets of lost love. And maids, of course. Maids always know."

Kate snorted and Jolie was satisfied.

The ocean voyage was perfect for four days, better than Jolie had expected, until they were one day out from Ireland. Then a heavy storm struck. The ship rolled and groaned, and sheets of rain poured on them. The terrible, punishing rain continued to fall when they reached Queenstown.

They were to part company with the Prescotts aboard ship, because the Prescotts were traveling on to London. Aunt Elizabeth would meet them at the Queenstown dock, they had been assured. Everything had been arranged.

As they left the ship, Jolie looked out at the bleak gray world ahead of her and wondered yet again if she had lost her mind.

Behind her, Kate said, "We're here!" in a voice that sounded as if she had just arrived in paradise.

Jolie, on the dock and feeling unsteady after several days at sea, thought that she was seeing the ugliest place on the face of the earth. A boy, barefoot and dressed in rags held together with strips of other rags, darted at her and demanded something from her in speech that was unintelligible to her. Appalled, she stepped back, but not quickly enough to prevent him from snatching at her coat pocket and ripping it half off before he ran away into the crowd, stuffing her coin purse inside his pants.

"Welcome to Ireland!" a slender, pretty woman called. She had been oblivious to the theft, and she held out her arms to Jolie. "Jolie, my dear, do you remember me? I'm your aunt Elizabeth."

"Do you want me to go after your purse?" Kate asked Jolie dutifully.

Jolie turned and saw her companion's face, alight with excitement as she looked around at the people and carriages and automobiles, everything colorless and depressing in the pouring rain. She shook her head and followed her aunt to the waiting carriage. "I didn't have much money in it," she told Kate.

Ireland. She could not wait to go home, even if it took another hideous train journey.

Part Three

A Sea So Far

CHAPTER 9

Kate

KATE SAID, "How do you do?" to Mrs. Elizabeth Cross when Jolie introduced them, but her attention was fixed on Jolie, who looked as if she were ready to faint. They were in the way of people hurrying about searching for friends and families, so Jolie's small, brisk aunt pulled them to one side, chattering at them all the time, her feathered black hat nodding briskly to emphasize her words. "It's always such a terrible journey . . . I can't think how you endured the train trip and still look so well . . . the Wardens' footmen are here for your belongings and they'll take them straight to the house where we'll be staying until tomorrow. . . ."

The black-clad woman managed to steer both of them through the crowd without delay, and with the help of a silent maid named Pocket, settled them in a large carriage and tucked heavy wool robes around them. "It's only a few blocks, but the weather turned foul, and I don't want you developing a chill. Heavens, but you're trembling, Jolie. Pocket, get out your smelling salts . . . No? Then take deep breaths, dear. Katè is it? My best friend's name is Kate. Pocket, run and tell the men that we're leaving now, and remind them that I won't tolerate dawdling. Run!"

The maid rushed away, and Mrs. Cross, assisted by a young, red-haired man, climbed into the coach and settled herself in the seat opposite Kate and Jolie.

"The Wardens have been wonderful. So kind of them to invite us to stay with them instead of in a hotel. We'll take the train to Dublin tomorrow, after you've had a chance to relax . . ."

Jolie sagged to the side and her eyes rolled back. Mrs. Cross let out a shriek, but Kate gestured to her to silence her and got up so that she could stretch Jolie out on the seat. Jolie's face was gray. Kate pulled off Jolie's hat and loosened her high collar, then felt on the side of her throat for her pulse. It was weak and rapid, fluttering under Kate's cold fingers.

"What is it?" Mrs. Cross demanded. "What's wrong with her?"

"She's very tired," Kate explained as she opened her medical bag on the seat next to Mrs. Cross and pulled out the smelling salts. She opened the little bottle and held it under Jolie's nose until she turned her head weakly and protested with "Don't!"

"Don't sit up," Kate said. "Just lie still. I'll prop up

your head." She grabbed two loose embroidered pillows and shoved them under Jolie's head.

Mrs. Cross looked as if she, too, might faint, so Kate said sharply, "She'll be all right if we can get her into bed as soon as possible."

She was not sure she told the truth. Jolie looked worse than she had ever seen her, but Dr. Logan had prepared her for times like this, and the two doctors at the hospital had spoken to her seriously—and privately—about Jolie. Kate's hands trembled as she measured out a dose of Jolie's heart medicine into the small cup she had taken from a corner of the bag. "Drink this quickly," she told Jolie, who raised her head a little higher and obeyed.

Mrs. Cross shouted out the coach window and demanded that they start for the house without delay. The coachman turned the horses out into the steady stream of traffic, earning himself curses from other drivers and the sea of pedestrians.

"There," Mrs. Cross said, satisfied. "I should have had Pocket ride with us instead of in the wagon with the luggage. She might have made herself useful."

Kate, busy unbuttoning Jolie's bodice, said, "No. I need room." The carriage jolted over a rough street and she had trouble keeping her balance. She pulled the blanket up a little higher and, underneath it, struggled first with the hooks on an under bodice and then with the heavier hooks on the front of Jolie's corset.

Finally Jolie drew a deep breath, held it, and sighed, "Thank goodness. That's better, Kate."

"Was she too tightly laced?" Mrs. Cross asked. "Girls! What can you be thinking?"

"What are any of us thinking when we torture our-selves with our clothing?" Kate said as she sat down next to her and wiped the cup clean before putting it back in the case. Jolie's garments contributed to her health problems, even though Kate had persuaded her to give up the extremely tight lacing she had preferred before. The design of women's clothing was bad enough to make perfectly healthy women wheeze and hobble. Kate, after a few conversations with nurses in the hospi-tal, had become convinced that women in poor health should dress very differently. But this was a subject she could not bring up very often to Jolie. Jolie might be-come suspicious. She might wonder about many things that her father would not face and the other doctors had decided to keep secret.

"Were you ill on the trip, Jolie?" Mrs. Cross asked.

"No, I was fine." But Kate knew now that she was lying. While she, Kate, was sick in bed with a cold, Jolie had been hiding the symptoms that would have alerted her companion to trouble.

"Well, all you need is a soft, warm bed and your din-ner on a tray," Mrs. Cross said. She sounded contented enough now. "The Wardens are planning a little dinner for you this evening, but that can be put off easily enough."

The trip was short, just as promised. The carriage pulled into the circular drive of a large stone house, and several servants rushed out into the rain to help the trav-elers inside. Kate paid little attention to them, for the challenge now was to get Jolie up a flight of stairs in as dignified a way as possible, and into bed. Jolie hated embarrassment, and any sign of her weakness or illness embarrassed her.

Kate closed Jolie's coat over her unbuttoned dress and almost lifted her out of the carriage. She kept her arm firmly around Jolie and, bearing all her weight, got her through the door, across the wide vestibule, and halfway up the stairs before she had to stop for a moment. Mrs. Cross was beside her instantly, and between the two of them, they helped—dragged—Jolie up the stairs and down the hall to the large room that had been prepared for her.

A woman introduced as Mrs. Warden, their hostess, hovered before and behind them, clucking and moaning. Kate knew she was kind, but she was in the way. However, nothing could be done. Mrs. Warden ordered maids this way and that. The fire and all the lamps in the room were lit. The heavy satin draperies were pulled against the bleak day, and the blankets on the high canopied bed turned back to reveal fresh sheets tucked in over a thick feather mattress.

The room, although large, was overcrowded. Mrs. Warden, Mrs. Cross, and two maids waited while Kate sat Jolie up on the edge of the bed and began removing her shoes.

"I wonder . . ." Jolie began breathlessly.

"Of course, you want a little privacy," Mrs. Cross said, and she steered her friend out the door as skillfully as she had steered the girls at the dock. The maids followed, and one of them shut the door quietly.

Jolie gasped for breath and would have fallen to the side again if Kate had not stopped her. "They're gone,"

Kate murmured. "You don't have to pretend with me. I hate myself for not seeing that you've been ill the whole time. This is my fault."

"I only started feeling really bad last night," Jolie said.

"Liar," Kate said. She had Jolie's stockings off now—her knees were swollen to twice their normal size!—and pulled her to her feet so that she could yank down her dress and petticoats at one time. She kicked the garments aside and threw Jolie's corset across the room angrily. "Why do you do it?" she whispered furiously. "You know that lacing yourself up even a little only makes it harder to breathe. You *know* that."

But Jolie did not answer. Kate eased her back on the bed and covered her with blankets. "When our trunks get here, I'll put you in a gown. For now, who cares what you're wearing? A chemise and bloomers are comfortable enough. I'm not going to let anyone back in, but I'm going to get tea for you. Here, let me put another pillow behind you. Don't talk! Don't say anything. I'll give you something nice to make you sleep as soon as we get the tea up here. Everything will be fine."

Kate left the room, to find Mrs. Cross waiting outside the door for her with a maid. Kate asked for tea and the maid hurried away. Mrs. Cross grabbed her arm and pulled her down the hall, to another bedroom. "Now listen to me, young Kate. I demand to know what is going on. Don't bother lying to me. What's wrong with Jolie?"

Mrs. Cross sat down on a small sofa and gestured to Kate to take the chair opposite her. "She's had a few problems since she had scarlet fever," Kate began, planning to recite what Dr. Logan had told her to say, if there were any difficulties. "Save your long explanations for doctors," he had said. "Everybody else becomes hysterical when someone mentions the word 'heart.'"

"What problems?" Mrs. Cross said. She unpinned her hat and put it on the sofa beside her, then started in on Kate, firing questions. "Exactly what problems? How long has she been ill? Was she ill on the trip? Do we need to have a doctor come to look at her? I think we do!"

Kate hesitated only a moment, then said, "Yes. If Mrs. Warden could send for one now, I'll explain the situation to him."

Mrs. Cross ran to the door, disappeared for a few moments, then came back and sat down again, her narrow face flushed. "She is calling the doctor on the telephone. Now tell me what is going on and don't mince words with me. Dr. Logan wrote a long letter to me about you, and I know you've had some nursing training—I suppose so that you can take better care of Jolie—but he never gave me the idea that she was an invalid!"

"She isn't!" Kate protested. "She's been doing so much better—"

"Better than *what?*" Mrs. Cross demanded.

Kate sighed. This woman was forceful, and she would never let up until she had the information she wanted.

"Jolie's heart was damaged by the fever. And she has fever in her joints, too, so that sometimes she has difficulty walking. She was doing much better, eating and gaining weight, which is why Dr. Logan thought that this was a good time to take the trip." That was part of the information, but it should be enough to satisfy Mrs. Cross.

The woman's eyes were a strange light brown, small and deeply set, and her hard gaze drilled holes into Kate. "I can't believe that her father would send her across an ocean when she has heart trouble. What's going on? Has he lost his mind?"

Kate sighed again and rubbed her cold hands together. There was nothing she could do now but tell the truth. "All right. Dr. Logan has not faced Jolie's illness. Two of the doctors at his hospital told me this. Dr. Logan believes that she is almost well. But he knows that Jolie can never marry—"

"Never marry!" Mrs. Cross exclaimed.

"She can't have children," Kate said. "Her heart is too weak."

"And he let her come to Ireland in that condition?" Mrs. Cross cried.

"He thinks that she can live a good life anyway. But he wanted to get her away from the house where her mother died. She can't seem to get over her loss . . ."

"Nor can I," Mrs. Cross said. Her eyes filled with tears.

"It's more than just sorrow," Kate said. "The doctor was concerned about her plans for the house. She would tell him how she would one day marry and have a little girl she would name Amy . . ."

"He hasn't told her that she can't marry?" The woman was horrified.

Kate shook her head. "And there was someone who interested her . . ."

"She's too young for that," Mrs. Cross said. She leaned back, satisfied. "If he just wanted to get her away from some young man, he need not have bothered. She couldn't marry anyone at seventeen."

Kate looked down at her hands, remembering the sheet of paper she had found in Jolie's wastebasket once, with "Mrs. David Fairfield" written dozens of times on it. "Dr. and Mrs. David Fairfield." Dr. Logan had admitted that he had told David what he would not tell Jolie—or fully accept himself. There would be no point in David's courting Jolie. There would never be a wedding.

"No, but she could wait for someone," Kate said. "Wait hopelessly. He didn't want her to do that. He wanted you to take her to London and Paris when you go, and show her the pleasures of travel, so that when she goes home in six months, she'll want to leave again for another place. He wanted to see her, but send her off again . . . At least, that was his plan."

"The man's a fool," Mrs. Cross said disgustedly. "A complete fool! If she's this sick, traveling will kill her. The strange food and bad water and diseases . . . What was he thinking?"

"Just that he loved her and wanted her to have some kind of life," Kate said simply. "He said there are unmarried women—and widows—who travel all the time. Women like you—and your friends."

Mrs. Cross burst into tears. "I can't believe this. I can't believe he would send away a dying child and expect me to preside over her last hours."

"It wasn't like that!" Kate said. She got to her feet, agitated. "She was doing so well! Everyone saw that. She was excited about having a trunk full of new clothes and making her friends jealous . . ." Kate nearly added that Jolie was proud of being an heiress to an estate, too, but mentioning it would be in bad taste.

Mrs. Cross leaned her head back and groaned. "Why didn't he consult other doctors? Experts? Why did he think that he knows everything?"

"He did. He just didn't believe them. He expects her back before Christmas, ready to go to Hawaii after January with their friends, the Prescotts, who are going. They brought us as far as Ireland, and they talk about travel and could interest her in it. He believed that it was all possible, and so did I. So did I, until today."

Mrs. Cross got up. "I'll have another bed brought into Jolie's room. Mrs. Warden had a room on the servants' floor made up for you, but obviously you are more than a servant—or a companion."

Kate flushed. "Yes." She thought about the bank account that would be waiting for her in San Francisco— if she completed the trip. She thought about her desire to see Ireland, and all she had seen so far was a conglomeration of rain-wet streets, horses and carriages, and strangers. If there were green fields unfolding somewhere, they were far from this place. Would she run away now, even if she could? No one could desert Jolie when she was so ill.

The maids had brought Jolie a tea tray but reported to Kate that she was asleep when they reached her room. A bed had been set up in a corner, and a quiet young maid was putting Kate's clothing away in a wardrobe.

"If there's anything else you want, miss . . ." she began.

Kate hushed her, looking quickly at Jolie, who did not stir. She led the maid into the hall and asked her if she could bring her something to eat—she was famished.

"The staff will have tea in an hour," the maid said politely. Staff. Of course. Kate would be considered only "staff" here.

"I want to eat in Miss Logan's room," she said. "Can you arrange that?"

"Of course," the maid said, pleased with the assignment, and she hurried away.

Kate went back to the room, changed from her traveling clothes into a loose wrapper, and brushed her hair. A bathroom adjoined the bedroom, and she longed for a long, hot soak. But she dared not leave Jolie alone, even for a moment.

Mrs. Warden knocked and entered with a short, elderly man. "This is Doctor Blackwood, our physician," she said. She left again, with only a long glance at the sleeping Jolie.

The doctor stood over the sleeping girl for a moment, and then said, "You're the nurse?"

"I've had some training," Kate said.

"Will you wake her?" he said. "I don't want to startle her. From her color, I'd say that she couldn't live through a fright. Strange room, strange old fellow in it, that's all she'd need to die right in front of us."

He smiled so kindly at Kate that she fell in love with him instantly. She touched Jolie's shoulder and said, "Jolie, you have a guest. Wake up now. Jolie."

Jolie woke slowly, reluctantly, but she, too, seemed charmed by the old man. She consented to being examined, and duly took deep breaths and coughed on demand. Kate showed him the contents of her leather bag, and he approved of most of the bottles and boxes, but one packet of powders caused him to shake his head.

"I'll give you something different," he said. "Something more effective. And I'll be back tomorrow morning. I don't want her moved out of this room. No food except liquids. Good strong soup. And I'd like her to take wine, every two hours."

"She hates it," Kate said.

The doctor turned and smiled down at Jolie. "Miss Logan, if I could only do those things I like and none of the things I do not like, then I would spend my evening by your bed telling you the stories my mother told me when I was a sick child. But I must go to a dinner and listen to people who are so dull that they should be shot, as a mercy to mankind." He lifted her hand, kissed it, and patted her head. "Do as I say."

When he left, Jolie said, "He's wonderful."

But Kate was looking at the packet of powder that he had given her, frowning over the instructions. "Yes," she said absently. "He's very nice."

She was not a nurse. All of this frightened her. She had had no idea, when she agreed to do as Dr. Logan asked, that she would be caring for someone as desperately ill as Jolie.

But then, neither had he. But the doctors at the hospital had known. They had thought the trip was madness. She had known that from the expressions on their faces.

Kate, Jolie, and Mrs. Cross spent four days at the Wardens' home, before Jolie was well enough to travel. Her recovery was considered nothing short of a miracle to the old doctor, but Kate saw something in Jolie that she had not seen before. An awareness of her condition.

They traveled to Dublin by train, taking up two compartments, and then they traveled by comfortable coach to Mrs. Cross's home.

It was called Green Hill. The stone house was large and graceful, part of it ancient, with new additions stretching back on both sides. It sat on a low, gentle hill overlooking unfolding green fields where sheep grazed, and a cluster of stone cottages that made up the village. Nearer to the house, along the road, there was a line of six whitewashed cottages, well kept, with doors painted bright blue, and small flower gardens under the back windows. Behind them sat a long, newer building with big windows to catch the light.

"These cottages are for the workers," Mrs. Cross said. "The factory is behind them. Isn't it beautiful? I'm carrying on the work, of course. We'll go see it as soon as you're ready, Jolie. Wait until you see . . ."

But Kate had seen that Jolie was not listening closely. She was looking out the coach window at the fields and smiling. "Beautiful," she whispered.

Kate smiled. This was what her mother had talked

about then, the green fields that stretched to a sea somewhere. The sun shone down on a perfect world, gentle
and saturated with peace. Jolie could regain her health
here, and together they would walk through those fields.

And one day, when Jolie was ready to leave for Paris
or Vienna or any of the places that her father had
dreamed she would see, Kate would slip away. Somewhere in Ireland, she would find her true place, her true
people.

Jolie would forgive her. Perhaps, one day, even Dr.
Logan would forgive her.

On a day like this one, Kate believed that anything
was possible. She glanced at Mrs. Cross and saw that
the woman was looking at her, too. They exchanged
smiles.

"I'm so glad I came," Kate heard Jolie say. "Father
was right to send me here."

CHAPTER 10

Jolie

"AH, THERE you are," Aunt Elizabeth said as she bustled into Jolie's bedroom, followed by two footmen carrying a small table.

Jolie, lying on the chaise by the windows that looked out over the distant village, smiled to herself. Where else would she be but in the bedroom where she had lived for the last six weeks? "I was watching Kate walking over to the factory," she said. "She's practically skipping. She loves watching the women work."

"And you're wearing one of the results," Aunt Elizabeth said, patting Jolie's shoulder. Jolie wore a loose cotton morning gown, embroidered by one of the women in the factory, who had made the gown according to a simple sketch of Kate's. "Put the table there, no, there," she said. The two men set the table down where she pointed and adjusted it one way and the other until Aunt Elizabeth nodded. "What do you think of this?"

Jolie said, "But it's yours, isn't it? What will you do when you want to paint?"

Aunt Elizabeth dismissed her question with a wave of one ringed hand. "I have plenty of places to work, if I want to start in again." The footmen left and Aunt Elizabeth picked up Jolie's sketchbook. "You've done some wonderful things in pencil and crayon. I've sent off the ones you wanted your father to have, but now I think it's time for you to use watercolors."

"I won't be any good," Jolie protested. "I never was when I was in school."

"Of course you're good," her aunt said firmly. "Your mother was a fine watercolorist when she was young. So was your grandmother. And I want you to see what I did when I was in Italy the last time." She hurried out of the room and came back promptly with a stack of sketchbooks. "Here," she said, and she put them in Jolie's lap. "Look these over. We spent most of December and January in Italy, in a friend's villa outside Rome. I painted and wrote these little notes on each page. See? They've been the best travel journals I ever kept. I'll get more blank books for you to record your stay in Ireland."

Jolie opened one book and saw a watercolor of a steep, sun-warmed cobbled street and the corner of a building, deep in shadow. "This is beautiful," she said. "I'll never learn to do anything like it."

"Oh, you will," Aunt Elizabeth said. "It's July. There's plenty of time. I've decided to write to your father and ask if you can spend the winter with me—in Italy."

Jolie looked up from the book, startled. "Oh, Aunt!" she exclaimed. "I can't do that. I must go home in November."

"We'll just see about that," Aunt Elizabeth said. "I'm counting on being able to persuade you to join me and my friends instead. Look through these books and then tell me that you don't want to see all of this for yourself. You're getting stronger every day. I'm sure that by October we can leave, and it's not a difficult journey. Heavens, it's not like that mad trip across America by train! We'll have lovely cabins on the ship, the best ones, of course, and pleasant stops along the way until we reach Rome. Then a few weeks there, and then an easy trip to the villa—and beyond. All that wonderful sunlight! The views! The people! And the food is straight from heaven itself. Then, in spring, we'll stay in Paris until the weather becomes unbearable there, and then we'll come home to Ireland." She bent over Jolie and brushed back a strand of her hair. "You can give your auntie a year out of your exciting life, can't you?"

Jolie, turning pages, and seeing the sunlit world her aunt loved so much, was tempted. But still, Father was alone in the house. What would he think if she changed her plans?

And what about Kate? She depended on the girl.

"Would we be bringing Kate?" she asked.

"Of course! I've grown accustomed to her tart tongue and bossy ways."

But Jolie, seeing Kate returning down the narrow road, wondered if Kate would want to see Italy. She seemed to love Ireland so much, even though sometimes she sighed over the letters she received from home. And Jolie was not certain that she wanted to see Italy, either. She was lonely for San Francisco. And there had been two letters from David since she arrived in Ireland, letters that gave her hope. He missed her and was concerned for her—he had said so in writing. She should be in San Francisco the next time he went home for a visit. Who could tell what the future held for them?

Her aunt left, to gather up her paints and brushes, and Jolie turned another page in the illustrated travel journal. Here was a landscape, a watercolor of a valley with planted fields and a scattering of small houses. The note at the bottom of the page said, "View from the highest overlook, Assisi." The valley shimmered in bright light, but a shadow fell across the lower part of the painting, as if the painter had been sitting under a sheltering tree.

It was so lovely. She could spend the winter in Italy and still be home in San Francisco when David reached there next June for summer vacation. But that was eleven months!

However, she would be completely well by then. She was getting stronger every day. The last doctor Aunt Elizabeth had called in—and his strange wife, who acted as his nurse—had done wonders. Especially the wife, with her exotic teas and soothing voice. "She's part witch," Aunt Elizabeth had said, laughing. "But she's wonderful."

Kate came in, damp red curls clinging to her forehead. "You should see what they're working on now," she said as she sat down beside the chaise. "A million yards of embroidered ribbon, and it looks like something fairies would make."

"A million yards?" Jolie repeated, smiling.

"You know what I mean," Kate said. "The women will be using it on petticoats, and I've asked for two for us. What's this table? What are all these books?"

"Aunt Elizabeth is trying to make an artist out of me. Here, look at her watercolors. She did them the last time she was in Italy, and she thinks I can learn to do something like them. She wants us to spend the winter in Italy, instead of going home."

Kate's head raised abruptly. "What do you mean?"

Jolie explained, surprised at Kate's reaction. She seemed frightened!

"And you want to do this?" Kate asked finally, when Jolie had finished.

"I'm not sure what I want," Jolie said. "Father expects me home in November. And I miss the house so much. But you don't want to leave Ireland, do you? I can tell how much you love it here."

Kate leaned back and sighed. "It was my mother's home. She was born in County Clare, and one of the women in the factory is from the same village and even remembers the family. Sometimes I think I knew what everything looked like in Ireland before I was even born."

"Your mother missed it?" Jolie asked.

Kate considered this, then shook her head. "I really don't know. I don't recall her saying that she did. My aunt said that Mother had always wanted to come to the United States and never looked back. But I remember Mother talking about the green hills and the cliffs and the sea. I'd like to see County Clare and look out across the ocean toward America, the way she did."

"We will, before we leave," Jolie said. "Aunt Elizabeth knows people everywhere. Surely she knows someone on the west coast we can visit for a few days."

"Don't ask her to do that," Kate said quickly. "I wasn't hinting that you had to go."

"But how would you get there?" Jolie asked. She felt the blood drain from her face. "You meant to go alone?" Her throat seemed to close, and she could not speak again. The expressions on Kate's face changed rapidly, and Jolie was certain that Kate was hiding something.

But Kate reached out and grabbed her hand. "Go without you? Of course not." She got to her feet then and brushed invisible lint from her dark blue skirt. "Goodness, what are we doing, carrying on like this? I have news, and I meant to tell you this right away. I asked Pocket if your aunt had an open landau and she does. It's time for you to get out of the house and ride around a bit. Wait until you see what's over the hill!"

Jolie interrupted. "Does Aunt Elizabeth know about this?"

Kate shook her head. "No. I wanted to be sure there was something comfortable for you, besides that awful big old coach—something that would let you get some sun on your face. And she doesn't much like ideas that she didn't come up with herself. So now you know that there is a landau, so I thought *you* could ask her."

Jolie laughed. "What a conspirator you are. The Irish could use your help with their political problems."

"I have enough to do right now," Kate said. "My other plan is working out a new wardrobe for you. You're so much more comfortable without stays. Admit it! What if you wore loose jackets over flared skirts, without stays or petticoats . . ."

"Without petticoats?" Jolie cried, and she burst out laughing. "You have gone mad."

"Well, maybe one petticoat, a slim one, under a simple flared skirt. And with a loose jacket over a loose shirtwaist. You'd have a chemise, naturally."

"I should hope so!" Jolie said. "I was expecting you to say that I'd be down to my altogether under that shirtwaist."

"No, that's what I'm planning for your aunt," Kate said, and she grinned over her shoulder as she left.

Jolie leaned back and laughed. Sometimes she almost liked Kate's ideas for clothing, even though she knew that she could not appear in public in one of these fantastic garments. Loose jackets and simple skirts! Aunt Elizabeth would never allow her out of the house dressed like that. And Jolie certainly couldn't go home to San Francisco—or on to Italy—in loose jackets, without a corset.

But Kate had a surprise for her. A week later, when Jolie felt stronger than she had since her illness, Kate presented her with a straight simple white shirt, a long boxy pale green linen jacket, and a matching skirt, slightly flared for comfortable walking. The jacket and shirt had been elaborately embroidered in a design of interlocking clover leaves, entwined with rosebuds, in a green slightly darker than the jacket. The clothes were not startling, even though they were different. When Jolie was dressed, it was impossible to tell if she wore a corset or not. If anything, the jacket looked as if it was only a little too big for her.

"And what do you care, anyway," Kate said. "You can breathe deeply, which you need to do. And move around more comfortably."

They were in Jolie's bedroom, watching Jolie's reflection in the long mirror on her wardrobe, with Aunt Elizabeth hovering in the background, alternately frowning and smiling.

"I love the color, Jolie," she said. "It's perfect for you. And the embroidery—I've never seen anything so beautiful. Kate, you must have put a charm on my women, to get one of them to do that. And unless one looked closely at the jacket—hmm. Well, Jolie will be sitting down in the landau. If we see someone and stop for introductions, she can simply lean forward a bit and no one will notice how loose the jacket is. Of course, she couldn't stand up."

Jolie, watching Kate from the corner of her eye, said, "Of course not, Aunt."

"And next week, when we have that little dinner to introduce you to our neighbors now that you're so well, you'll wear something—ahem!—different."

"Something that won't shock anyone, Aunt," Jolie agreed.

But Kate was muttering, and Jolie wondered if Kate had plans for her clothing at the dinner party, too.

The drive was everything Jolie had hoped it would be. After Kate and Pocket helped her downstairs and got her settled in the landau, with Aunt Elizabeth hovering and fussing around them, the coachman drove the four women through the village and out into the country-side. The sun was warm, and the sky was a deep, clear blue. Wildflowers bloomed in crevices in the rock walls that divided the fields, and roses bloomed along the road. Once they stopped for several minutes while a farmer drove a flock of sheep before them, finally turn-ing them into a rolling field that stretched to the hori-zon, where a tall tower stood alone, a thousand-year-old reminder of invasions nearly forgotten. Jolie watched Kate listening intently to Aunt Elizabeth's small history lesson. *How she loves it here,* she thought. *What stories she'll bring back to her friends.*

Often, people beside the road bobbed their heads as the landau passed, and Aunt Elizabeth called out greet-ings to them by name. Jolie knew that the woman gen-uinely cared about the villagers and the people at the farms, even though they would never be invited inside the house.

Kate had very definite—and very American—views about the class distinction in Ireland, but Aunt Eliza-beth was comfortable with it. Her husband had believed that one day Ireland would be independent from England and was glad for it. He built the factory to help Irish women, whom he believed to be the most unfortunate anywhere. Only women were employed in it, creating fine undergarments and table linens out of fabrics woven in a mill he owned. It had been his idea to include a small card with each one, bearing the words, "Made by the Sisters of Green Hill." He had intended, Aunt Elizabeth had reported, that the customers in London would think that the delicate linens had been made by nuns. "It was his effort at breaking down the barriers between the churches," she had said. "He believed that what they didn't know would be good for them. Everybody likes to imagine that their linens were embroidered by nuns, even if they hate Catholics."

But Kate once seethed when Jolie and she were alone because the factory women were required to wear uniforms—neat dark blue linen dresses with white aprons—and caps covering their hair. "What difference does it matter what they wear?" she had asked.

"My aunt gives them the clothes," Jolie had said. "They've never had such nice things. I imagine that they're grateful, Kate! You're so American!"

Kate had been only partly mollified by that, Jolie remembered. Why did she care so much? The women were paid well, as much as—or more than—most of the men in the area earned in the mill. Sometimes Jolie wondered if Kate's interest in what went on in Ireland went deeper than just enjoying a visit in the place where her mother had been born. Yes, she loved Ireland. But didn't she love San Francisco even more? How could you not love it more? The climate was more dependable—although Kate would hoot at that and remind her of the awful, cold summer fogs—and one could count on most of the rain falling during a few weeks of the year. And there were the theaters and restaurants—although if she brought them up, Kate would remind her that Dublin had many fine theaters, which they would investigate as soon as Jolie was well enough.

The landau had turned toward home and Jolie was tired. She leaned back and closed her eyes. Kate. What was going on in her mind?

"Are you all right, Jolie?" Aunt Elizabeth asked. "Oh, you're too tired. I was afraid of this."

Jolie sat up and smiled. "I'm fine. I've loved every moment of this, and I hope you'll let me do it again. I need the fresh air, and everything is so lovely."

"You shall do it whenever you like," Aunt Elizabeth said. "But now, let's get you in the house and up to your room. And I think I'll call Dr. Bridewell in, just to make sure you're all right."

"Call Mrs. Bridewell instead," Jolie said. Even as she asked for the doctor's wife, she felt Kate nudge her in warning.

"I think the doctor might be better," Aunt Elizabeth said firmly. "I know his wife has been very helpful to you—and she doesn't do anything he doesn't want her to do—but she's the strangest creature. That hair. Sometimes I expect to find brambles tangled in it."

Both Jolie and Kate laughed. Mrs. Bridewell was ageless, with long curly hair streaked with gray, which she left loose and hanging over her shoulders. She always wore a cape with a dozen pockets sewn into it, both inside and out, over a dark dress. She was never seen without a tapestry bag, in which she carried packets of the teas she prepared for Jolie, as well as scraps of paper that she left under Jolie's pillow, scraps with strange symbols drawn on them in colored ink. Jolie had always been careful to remove the papers before Aunt Elizabeth or one of the maids saw them. She and Kate had marveled over them and promised each other that they would ask the woman what they meant the next time she came. But neither of them did. There was something about her that was so mysterious that they were cautious in her presence.

Pocket and Kate got Jolie upstairs again without much trouble, and Pocket went down for a tea tray while Kate got Jolie out of her new clothing and into a night-gown.

"Tea in bed, and I'll read you to sleep until Dr. Bridewell gets here," Kate said.

"That sounds good," Jolie said. "But I had a wonderful time. I felt better than I've felt since before I had scarlet fever."

"Good," Kate said. "Now rest until tea gets here, and think of what you'll say this winter when a handsome Italian prince proposes marriage to you."

Jolie laughed. "So you want to go," she said.

"I didn't say that," Kate said. "It's just something to dream about, isn't it?"

Jolie leaned back into the soft pillows and smiled. "You like the idea. I'm on to all your tricks, Kate," she said.

She thought she heard Kate say, "I hope not," but

she was not sure, and before she could ask, Kate had walked out, carrying her new clothes. "I'll get someone to press these," she said as she closed the door.

Pocket came with the tea, and Kate returned, carrying a vase of roses. "Your aunt sent these up, to remind you of your drive. Now I'll pour our tea and then we'll pick up in the book where we left it yesterday. Let's see ... wasn't the duchess about to elope with the gamekeeper?"

"Kate, have you ever considered reading something more enlightening?" Jolie asked as she accepted her cup. She was smiling.

"No. Have you?"

"Never," Jolie said. She laughed aloud. "Read to me about the duchess and the mysterious French gamekeeper."

This was so pleasant. Kate and Aunt Elizabeth were wonderful companions. Perhaps they could travel together. For a while, at least.

CHAPTER 11

Kate

KATE WATCHED Jolie flourish in warm August, growing stronger and more animated every day. Her aunt gave several small parties for her, and Jolie made friends with young people from the nearby estates. The young American with her obviously Irish companion fascinated the young women and intrigued the young men, and their parents accepted her in spite of her American ways. Jolie had new friends now, who admired her clothes and painting, and who were quick to make allowances for her still fragile condition. She was not expected to walk the short distance to the other side of the village for tea with Helena Proctor and her mother—the Proctors sent a pretty carriage heaped with blue silk cushions and pulled by a pair of small white horses. The

Smith-Shermans asked her to dinner and made arrangements for her and Kate to spend the night, rather than return five miles home after dark in a carriage. Dr. Bridewell came only once during the month, and not because he had been called for, but because he was curious about her well-being. He was delighted, he told her. To Kate, though, he expressed a certain reserve and warned her against allowing Jolie to tire herself.

His wife, however, drifted in and out of Jolie's bedroom frequently, bringing strange teas and soda bread, and once, a small pot of crushed herbs, strongly scented, to leave open beside her bed if she had difficulty sleeping. To Kate, Mrs. Bridewell's face seemed too carefully neutral, but the woman said nothing. Kate began to believe that Jolie was regaining her health, and she wrote optimistic letters to Dr. Logan.

The September weather was changeable, bright sunlight one day and light, silver rain the next. On the gray days, mists formed in the bogs and valleys and rolled up toward the big house, rising mystically, delicately, shrouding everything. Kate chose such a day to search out Mrs. Bridewell. Jolie had been in Dublin with her aunt for a week and was not due back for several more days. It was her first trip without Kate.

Kate found the doctor's witch-wife at home, sitting placidly in a gazebo at the edge of the pasture where several mares grazed with their colts. Mrs. Bridewell was holding a long green thread in her lap, and she manipulated it between her fingers, somehow turning the thread into a cord. Next to her on the wooden bench lay a dozen other cords, made of different colors. In a basket at her feet, spools of thread were tumbled in with scraps of lace and ribbon, dried flowers and ferns, and a bundle of fragile sticks. The woman's hair fell loose over her shoulders, crisp and curly, and her calm gray eyes studied Kate for a long moment before she spoke.

"Did you find Galway to your liking?" she asked. Mrs. Cross had given Kate permission to accompany Mrs. McNeil and Miss Cooley, from the factory, to Galway for two days during Jolie's absence, where they bought laces from women who made them in their cottages.

Kate smiled. "I saw the village where my mother was born, although it's deserted now, not much more than half a dozen cottages without roofs or doors. Mrs. McNeil warned me that I'd be disappointed, and I admit that I was. But I loved seeing the places where Mother must have walked—and the beautiful fields and the sea. She spoke of them so often." She did not add that when she stood on a cliff looking out over the rough sea, she thought for a moment that she could see the golden hills of San Francisco in the distance, and her heart seemed to jump in her chest. But that was impossible—San Francisco was on the other side of the world—and the vision had only lasted for a moment, passing so quickly that she barely experienced it. She pushed it out of her thoughts firmly.

There was a stool opposite the bench, and Mrs. Bridewell indicated that she wanted Kate to sit there. The cord grew in length, without the woman ever looking at it. "You're here to talk about Jolie," she said.

"Before she left, she seemed to feel better than ever.

I'd never seen her like that, so animated, laughing at everything. She was excited about going to Dublin to visit her aunt's friends. They had planned parties and visits to theaters. Pocket went with them, and she's good with Jolie." Kate hesitated a moment. "But . . . I wanted to ask you something."

Mrs. Bridewell nodded. Rain had begun falling, a light shower at first, and then a hard rain. A small white dog came into the gazebo and climbed into the basket with the spools and laces, circled, then lay down abruptly with a sigh. Mrs. Bridewell smiled down at him.

"First, let me ask *you* something," Mrs. Bridewell said as she completed the cord and lay it across her lap. "Do you see yourself staying in Ireland?" she said quietly.

Kate was accustomed to the woman reading her mind, but this time she shook her head, wincing. "I love it here," she whispered. "I want to live my life in my mother's land, but . . ."

"She was called away to a different land, the one where she truly belonged," Mrs. Bridewell said.

"I don't want to go back to California," Kate began. Memories flared, of broken buildings, fire, ashes, weeping people searching through rubble, horses sweating and dying by the thousands while the city rose again. "This place is so peaceful, so gentle . . ." Kate said brokenly, her eyes on the horses in the pasture, grazing quietly in the rain.

Mrs. Bridewell laughed. "If it's peace you want, you won't be finding it here. Not in your lifetime. Your mother cast her lot with America, where there are battles enough to fight that you understand better than any going on here. Our struggle will take place in our heart's core. Yours will come from choosing the song that your heart will sing."

The maid who had brought Kate to the gazebo returned now, carrying a tray with a coffeepot, two mugs, and a plate of sliced soda bread. She set it on a small table that she pulled close to Mrs. Bridewell, and then she left, running, holding her hands over her head to protect her hair from the rain.

Mrs. Bridewell poured coffee for both of them. "You wanted to ask about Jolie," she said. "But your fate is tangled with hers now, and what happens to her will make your decision for you."

Kate drank coffee and waited. Outside, the rain glimmered in a sudden slant of light that broke through the clouds.

"My mother told me about her mother's favorite apple tree," Mrs. Bridewell said. "It was an old tree, and one year it bloomed better than it had in anyone's memory. Everyone in the village came to see it, and people from miles around came, too. No one had ever seen anything like it. But my grandmother stood under it and cried, because she knew it was dying. It gave them more apples than it ever had, and people told her she was wrong, that the tree was not dying. Look at it, they would say. See how it bears. But she knew that a dying tree will put out blossoms and fruit desperately, to keep its own life going, through its offspring."

Kate stared at her, uncomprehending.

"And so it is with many people. In the last days, they flower and bear fruit. Jolie seems well to you and to her aunt, who adores her, and to everyone else. But Dr. Bridewell knows. And I know. And you know, yes, you do."

"Her paintings, her writings . . ." Kate began. She swallowed hard. "Are those the fruit?"

Mrs. Bridewell put down her mug and picked up the green cord from her lap. "When I heard you were coming—" she began.

"I didn't telephone you," Kate interrupted.

"When I heard you were coming," Mrs. Bridewell began again, "I made a life cord for you. Some wear them around their necks, under their clothing."

Kate took the cord. It felt warm in her hand. It had a loop on one end and a small thread button on the other. She fastened it around her neck and tucked it under her high collar. "Thank you," she said. "Couldn't you make one for Jolie?"

Mrs. Bridewell was silent. When Kate looked up, she saw the woman's tears falling. Her small dog whined suddenly and leaped into her lap, snuggling under her arm. Kate sobbed harshly and covered her face with her hands.

"You might be wrong," she said.

"Of course," Mrs. Bridewell said. "I've prayed at the holy place every morning that I am wrong."

Kate knew the place she meant. In the woods, there was a spring where Mrs. Bridewell had taken her once. It bubbled out in a thin trickle from between rocks carved with coils, one after the other, like mazes side by side. The doctor's wife could not explain the carvings, except to say that they were older than humans, and meant to call to the first people, the ones who would serve the "woman in the well." She did not explain that, either, and Kate did not ask. Sometimes Mrs. Bridewell frightened her. Other times she felt that she was in the presence of a holy woman.

"I write to Jolie's father every week," Kate said. "I've been telling him how well she has been. And she has written to him, explaining that she wants to go to Italy with her aunt instead of home in November. He'll be happy. He wants her to become a world traveler, to make that her life, even though he'll miss her." Kate paused, then went on. "He only meant me to see her through her first trip."

Mrs. Bridewell sighed and stroked the dog's head. "The journey back to San Francisco is harder than the one to Italy. Italy would be a better idea for Jolie."

Kate shut her eyes tightly and bit her lip. "I should go to Italy with her, then."

"What have you told her?"

Kate looked up and shrugged helplessly. "That I would go. That I want to. I haven't told her that I want to stay here, or that I was planning to run away from her here. That had been my plan from the beginning, but she became so ill . . . she needed me so much."

"If your heart is set on Ireland, then you can return here afterward . . ."

"You mean that she won't return from Italy," Kate said.

"I mean that her time is nearly up, whether here or in Italy I cannot say."

- *Kate* -

Kate groaned. "I should stay with her then."

"And afterward?"

Kate shook her head. "I'll come back here, I suppose. I want to live here, one way or another, in spite of what you said. I don't see how I can leave this place behind, now that I've seen it."

"It's not what you think," Mrs. Bridewell cautioned. "Listen to me. The strength that is needed here is different from the strength that you have. Your strength is in building. Creating."

"And what kind of strength would I need to stay here?" Kate asked angrily.

"The strength of a warrior," Mrs. Bridewell said. "You are not Irish, Kate. You are an American girl from a golden place where cities are springing up everywhere, where ideas for building and creating are desperately needed. I hear the women in the factory talking about you. You so young and so full of ideas, so joyful when they're teaching you—you'll take home what you've found and turn it into something more wonderful than you can imagine now. That is what I see for you."

"But my mother . . ."

"She was called away from Ireland. You know that now. You've seen the golden hills yourself."

"You've read my mind," Kate said, chilled.

"No, I read your heart. You're too young to keep it hidden from those who love you and too innocent to keep it hidden from enemies. Don't make any."

Kate left a few minutes later, unsatisfied, and walked swiftly toward home. But as she passed the factory, she decided to go into the big workroom and see what the

· 173 ·

women were doing. Most of them greeted her kindly, but a few were still reserved around this talkative American. She was the servant of a guest at the big house, and even though they owed their jobs and cottages to the Cross family, they harbored resentment against the "outsiders." The women who had become her friends showed her the tablecloths they were working on that day, covered with openwork embroidery, white on white.

"I sent two of the appliquéd ones to San Francisco, to my friend," she told them. "And I decided at the last minute to put in bloomers and a petticoat, too. Both she and my aunt know people working in the big department stores in San Francisco. They'll love your work. The Sisters of Green Hill will be famous one day."

"Imagine American women wearing our bloomers," one woman said, laughing.

"Imagine American women paying us for them," another said. "That will be the best part."

Kate hurried toward the house, then, smiling to herself. Jolie's aunt had been enthusiastic about Kate's suggestion that she send some of the "Sisters'" work to San Francisco. Ellen had never given up her hope to have her own shop one day, and she had told Aunt Grace about it finally, something that Aunt Grace mentioned frequently in her letters. "Someday you and Ellen will have a shop," Aunt Grace would write. Grimly, Kate thought about the money waiting for her in the San Francisco bank. She could not help but feel guilty.

Should someone tell Dr. Logan that Jolie might not live much longer? He would be devastated, and what was the point? Mrs. Bridewell might be wrong. She admitted even praying that she *was* wrong. What should be done? Kate did not know.

Near the end of the road, by the gates that led to the big house, she passed an apple tree loaded with ripe fruit. Four barefoot young children were picking apples and squabbling among themselves. They were soaked to the skin from the rain, and their clothes were little better than rags held together with bits of string and shreds of other rags. Some of the village children appeared to be without parents, and Kate sometimes wondered if a few of them had any families at all. But when she asked the women in the factory about this, they turned silent and visibly hostile. It was at times like that when Kate understood how much of an outsider she would always be here.

When she had asked Mrs. Cross about the children, the woman had shrugged and said, "There's little anyone can do. We tried. You can't force someone to care about their children. If only someone would close the pubs! It's always made me ill to watch some of them spend what little money they have on drink. And if you give the mothers money for the children, the men might take it away from them. The best we could manage was to save some of the unmarried women and a few of the widows. And for years everyone laughed at us. 'The Sisters of Green Hill.' Oh, we were a great source of amusement, until they saw that the factory was a success. But did anyone else want to try? Of course not. The men use up their energy in hating the English and me—an American—and the women use up their energy giving birth to children they can't care for." She gave

Kate a sharp, discerning look. "And is it so different among the poor in America? Of course not. Women need to help other women, and who knows why they will not."

Kate never had brought up the subject again.

She left the children behind and hurried to the front door, knowing that Pocket would have a coal fire burning in the bedroom for her, and there was the promise of a good dinner in the staff dining room later on.

At the great front door, she looked back once at the misted hills and fragile curtain of rain. This land should be my home, she thought. But is it?

Jolie returned in high spirits, with new clothes and books, and an absurd doll she said reminded her of Kate. The china doll had green eyes that moved and a thick mop of curly red hair. Jolie set it on one of the windowsills in the bedroom and said, "We'll call her Kitty. Now come and see the hat I got for you. It will be perfect for Italy."

Her clear, pale skin glowed with health. Behind her glasses, her eyes shone. Her hair was lustrous and smooth. She weighed so much more than she had that the dresses she had brought from San Francisco had to be let out at the seams.

Kate tried on the neat straw hat with rosebuds around the rim. "It *is* perfect," she said, automatically wondering what Ellen would think of it and if she would ask to borrow it. "How did everything go? I warned you not to lace up too tightly, but I see that you have."

"I've been fine!" Jolie exclaimed. "I haven't had any

problems at all. I wasn't short of breath even once, and look!" She pulled up her skirts to show Kate her knees. "They aren't swollen anymore. They don't hurt." She dropped her skirts and pulled a sketchbook from her small suitcase. "Wait until you see the sketches I made of Trinity College!"

Kate forced herself to smile, but all she could think about was the apple tree, laden with fruit.

In a few days, Jolie developed a heavy cold. Mrs. Cross said that everyone in the house where they had stayed had come down with colds, but no one seemed to be particularly sick. But Kate asked her to send for Doctor Bridewell, and he came within an hour, a little before four o'clock.

Kate had put Jolie to bed early in the day, but she had grown steadily worse, and now, in late afternoon, she was burning with fever. Mrs. Cross and Kate stood back while Dr. Bridewell examined Jolie, listening to her chest for a long time. At last he eased her back onto her pillows again and gestured to Mrs. Cross to follow him out to the hall.

"Her lungs are inflamed," he said. "Her heart is struggling. This is very serious, but there is little I can do. Poltices for her chest and feet to try to sweat it out of her. Something to soothe the cough. But there is no cure, and I tell you this frankly. She will get well in her own time—or she will not."

Mrs. Cross took a step back. "It's that serious? But we thought it was just a simple cold."

"No. For someone without heart trouble, this would

be only an inconvenience. But every inflammation costs Miss Logan's heart the strength it needs to keep beating. I'll come back tonight, but there isn't much more I can do. Keep her as warm as she will tolerate, give her hot fluids, and keep her quiet."

"Should I give her some of the sleeping powder?" Kate asked.

"No, not under any circumstances. It will only weaken her heart even more."

He was sorry, he said, but they would have to wait and let time tell them how this would turn out.

After he left, Mrs. Cross said angrily that the doctor was behaving as if he thought Jolie was dying. "I have half a mind to call back Dr. Linnington," she said. "Jolie likes Dr. Bridewell better, but it can't hurt to see what the man says."

Kate agreed. At that point, the more doctors the better. Call them all, from there to Dublin and even farther. Jolie must not die like this, without warning, of nothing more than a cold! Not when she had been feeling so well, looking so well.

All around the room, Jolie's watercolors hung like jewels. She had pinned them up casually, but Kate would not let her take them down. Both she and Mrs. Cross had sent a few to Dr. Logan, and one had even found its way to David Fairfield, at Harvard Medical School in Boston.

Nothing bad is going to happen, Kate thought furiously. She rang for the maid, asked for more coal, and built up the fire. Against Jolie's protests, she fed her hot broth, spoonful by spoonful. Pocket brought hot stones wrapped in flannel from the kitchen to keep Jolie's feet warm. Mrs. Cross carried up a vase filled with the last roses from the south garden, mixed in with white daisies.

But Jolie's breathing whistled in her chest, and the coughing spasms left her weak, with blue lips and eyes rolled back in her head.

The doctor came and went, came and went, for five days. At one point Kate was certain that Jolie was near death. Not particularly religious, she dug through her drawers until she found the rosary that Aunt Grace had sent with her, and she sat by Jolie's bed, whispering Hail Marys for hours at a time.

But Jolie began to recover on the sixth day, and by early afternoon, she could sit up without help and hold her own water glass to her mouth.

"Kate," she said, her voice cracked and weak. "I don't think I'll be able to go to Ireland after all."

Kate stared. What was Jolie talking about?

Jolie handed Kate the glass and added, "Tell Father that I'm so very sorry to disappoint him." She fell back then, at first into what Kate thought was a faint. But she was sleeping.

Sleeping!

Kate sat by her for an hour, listening to her breathe, and when Jolie woke again, she asked to see Aunt Elizabeth.

Kate ran to get her, thankful that Jolie was no longer delirious. She could be mending now. She could truly be getting well. She had to be!

Mrs. Cross followed Kate back to the bedroom and

stood beside the bed, wringing her hands and blinking anxiously.

Jolie looked up at her, smiling, her eyes sunken, her skin sallow and pulled tight across her cheekbones. "When were we planning to leave for Italy?" she asked. "I'll be ready. You can't imagine how much better I'm feeling."

Mrs. Cross said, "I can see that, dear. I can see how much better you are."

But when she and Kate went back to the hall, she whispered, "Come to my room."

Kate followed wearily and closed the door behind them. Mrs. Cross turned immediately and said, "She's *not* better. We must get a different doctor. Or as many doctors as it takes until something is done. Look at her skin! Her eyes! And her hands, how they shake! What does all this mean, except that she is dying?"

"It means that her heart is not strong enough," Kate said sadly. "Yes, call the other doctors. Dr. Bridewell won't mind. And call his wife, too. Jolie likes her, and her teas always seemed to help."

The doctors came one by one, contradicted one another, prescribed new treatments and new medicines. The only one who actually helped Jolie was Mrs. Bridewell, with her mysterious teas and songs and soft whispers. And small scraps of paper tucked lovingly under Jolie's pillow each evening.

Jolie rallied again and was out of bed by the end of October. She even came downstairs one day, to oversee Kate's packing of a box of linens to be sent to San Francisco.

"Be sure that Ellen and your aunt know that I chose

most of these things," Jolie said. She was bracing herself against the back of a chair and refused to sit down. "There, see those petticoats with the embroidered ribbons? I wanted those put in the box with a note. I know my friends will snap them up the instant they see them. And I'll never tell that the 'Sisters' aren't real nuns. What a great joke I'll have on them when I get back next year."

Kate and Mrs. Cross exchanged a quick glance. Jolie saw it and said, "Perhaps I'm not going to Italy next month the way we'd planned, but surely I'll be ready by January."

"Surely you will," Mrs. Cross said stoutly.

"But," Jolie said, "Kate must go home to San Francisco next month, as we had planned all along."

"What?" Kate exclaimed, shocked.

"Oh, yes, Kate," Jolie said composedly. She finally let herself down into the chair. "I have it all worked out, and I've written to Father about it. I knew you were not very enthusiastic about going to Italy. But I am, you see. The more I think about it, the more wonderful it sounds. Aunt and I will make the trip after Christmas, and I'll write you and tell you all about it. Then next summer, when she and I go to San Francisco, I'll show you all my watercolors. And I'll bring you all sorts of surprises."

Kate still could only stare. "You're sending me home?" she asked finally.

"Yes, I am definitely sending you back to California," Jolie said. "You should be with your friends again. Aunt and I will become two lady travelers who write wonderful letters home to make everyone jealous. Who knows where we will go next? I've been looking through the travel books in the library, and I think I'd like to see some exotic tropical place. What do you think, Aunt Elizabeth?"

Mrs. Cross's face was frozen into a smiling mask. "A long South Seas voyage, dear? Is that what you want? Then you'll have it. Now let's get you upstairs for a little rest. Pocket, give us a hand."

Kate watched while Mrs. Cross and Pocket half-carried Jolie up the stairs.

Why is she doing this? she thought. Why is she sending me home to San Francisco?

And then she understood. Because Jolie would not be going home to California herself, not ever. She would never see her house again. And now she knew it.

Kate stayed downstairs until she was certain that Jolie was asleep, and then she climbed the stairs slowly. She was astonished to find Mrs. Bridewell on the upper landing.

"What are you doing here?" she asked.

"Pocket brought me up the back stairs," she said.

"Have you seen Jolie?"

Mrs. Bridewell nodded. "We'll be spending more time together. She'll like the old stories about the saints, and the older ones about the real people of Ireland. She's drawing closer to them now."

"You didn't tell the stories to me," Kate said.

"No, I didn't," Mrs. Bridewell said. She reached out and took Kate's hand and pressed something into her palm. "For later," she said.

Then she turned and hurried down the hall to the back stairs.

Kate opened her hand and looked down at a green bead, exactly like the one her mother had once given her, a green bead carved with a spiral. Suddenly she remembered the hills surrounding San Francisco, green in early spring, glowing with wildflowers in summer. She clenched the bead hard until her hand ached.

Before she went to bed, she strung it on the green cord and tucked it under the collar of her nightgown, next to her skin.

I'm going home, she thought, barely realizing that she was smiling even as she wept.

CHAPTER 12

Jolie

AN EARLY November storm had torn down the old apple tree by the gates, and Jolie watched from her window while the elated people from the village cut up the tree and carried it away, all within an hour. Wood was so precious to them, and to have a wood fire instead of a peat fire must have been an unimaginable treat. Jolie, with her elbows propped on her table, smiled as she watched the figures disappearing down the rough road.

There was Kate, windblown, her red hair loose from her braid, walking back from the factory with two of the women workers who carried a straw hamper between them. Kate was taking dozens of linen pieces home to San Francisco, and she was leaving in only three days.

Three days! Jolie got up carefully and moved to her

chaise. For a few moments, after she sat down, she concentrated on breathing. It helped to arch her back and
push against the chaise arms, but lately she had grown
so much weaker. How much more could she endure? she
wondered. But then she shook her head and made herself smile. Kate must not see her feeling discouraged.

Returning to California, Kate would follow the
route planned last spring by Father and Peter Prescott,
with only a few changes. She, Jolie, would not be going,
so Pocket and one of the footmen would accompany
Kate as far as Queenstown, where she would board the
ocean liner and, afterward, be in the care of the
Prescotts. They already would have boarded in England.
Then they would return to New York to begin the long
trip across the country, and arrive in San Francisco at
last. The ruffled bay, the gentle hills . . .

Jolie pressed her hands against her eyes and took a
deep breath. Don't cry, she told herself. Kate will be here
in a minute.

When Kate came into the bedroom, Jolie was writing another letter to her father. She looked up, pretending surprise. "Did you get everything you wanted?" she
asked.

"All that and more," Kate said. "Those darling
women! They made me half a dozen petticoats as a surprise, with my monogram on every one. That's almost a
lifetime supply."

"For you it will be," Jolie said, laughing. "Especially
if you're going to start wearing trousers—as you say you
will."

Kate shook rain off her coat and hung it over her

wardrobe door to dry. "I'm tempted to do it. Whenever I think about that train ride, I could scream. Wouldn't trousers have been more comfortable? Admit it. We could have been striding about, stepping over bundles and children and the occasional inebriated traveling salesman, breathing deeply, flexing our muscles, altogether perfect pictures of young womanhood."

Jolie raised her hands in surrender. "I admit everything. But I like the traveling suit you made for yourself. Corduroy velvet was a wonderful idea, and gray is a perfect color. Show it to me again."

Kate looked pleased as she pulled the suit out of the wardrobe and held it up. The jacket was boxy and rather long, and the skirt was flared, with an inverted pleat in front to make walking easier. Both the jacket and skirt had large pockets, and she had sewn hidden pockets inside the jacket. "No ragamuffin is going to rob *me* on the dock," she had told Jolie.

"I almost envy you traveling without corsets or stays sewn into your clothes," Jolie said.

"And my corsets will stay in my trunk until I'm home," Kate said. "I don't know what Aunt Grace will say when she finds out that I crossed half of the world without them. But it will be too late, then."

"Aunt Elizabeth would have me locked in my stateroom if I try something like that on our voyage to Italy," Jolie said. "She's already hinted that I'm not to get ideas from you about travel clothes. She's certain that I'll attract all sorts of attention from Italian noblemen *if* I have the proper clothes."

Kate, busy at the wardrobe, said, "And would you

like that?" Her voice was muffled, probably just because of the garments that half-buried her.

"Attention from noblemen? Certainly. Wouldn't Merry Johnson go mad with jealousy if I went home next summer for a month with a prince in tow?"

Kate closed the wardrobe doors. Clearing her throat, she said, "She would go mad with jealousy even if you came home with a widowed street singer and his ten children. But either way, your father would hate it. You know he would. He surely has a dozen nice blond American suitors lined up for you. Handsome, of course. All bookworms with better taste in books than yours. But don't you let him persuade you of anything. Probably there are already rumors about you in Rome among the idle rich in the piazzas. Sonnets are being composed and love songs written in your honor."

Jolie laughed. "If Father could have his way, I would spend years in Europe, never even looking at a man, and then come home some day and fuss over him for the rest of his life. I've been pestering him to tell me about the house, but he never remembers to write about it. Mrs. Conner must have changed all the bedrooms for winter by now. I meant to write her and make sure that she put the scarlet bedspread on Mother's bed."

"I'll remind her," Kate said. "I'll see her as soon as I can when I get back. She'll want a full report about you."

"Well, you can tell her everything except how I've been dressed," Jolie said. "She would never approve. You look tired. Why don't you ask Pocket to get us something to eat?"

Kate shook her head. "I don't have time, but if *you're* hungry . . ." She waited while Jolie considered this, then added, "Never mind. I'll ask that she bring something up. I want you to eat more."

She rushed out, then, calling for Pocket, and Jolie heard her running downstairs. A few minutes later, Pocket appeared with a tray of sliced bread and cake and a pot of tea. "Kate says that she won't be up for a while. She's gluing labels on her luggage. We told her we would do it, but she won't let anyone help her with anything."

"If you saw how people's belongings are handled on the trains, you wouldn't wonder that she wants to be sure that the labels are stuck on. Thanks, Pocket, but I think I'll have this in bed. Would you give me a hand? And then bring me my writing case."

Pocket helped her to her feet and clucked over her as she tucked her in bed. "Should I call Kate? Mrs. Cross?"

"No, I just want my tea and cake, and then I'll write a few letters—and perhaps take a short nap. Please close the door when you leave. Kate has such a way of barging in . . ." She laughed, and Pocket laughed a little, too.

As soon as the maid was out of the room, Jolie pushed the tray away. She had to finish writing to Father, because Kate was going to take the letter with her. And then she would write to Kate. That letter would be trusted to the mail, and reach home around the same time Kate did, or perhaps a little later. It did not matter. There were things she had to say to Kate, but she could not say them in person.

Propped up in bed, she wrote a loving paragraph to her father, thanking him for a lifetime of affection and care, and then sealed the envelope that she had already addressed to him. She took another sheet of paper from her small writing case and wrote to David Fairfield, thanking him for the book of poetry he had sent. The letter was only two lines long and would go in the post, along with Kate's. She signed it, "Affectionately, Jolie Knight Logan."

Before she folded the sheet and slipped it into an envelope, she looked out the window for a long time. The rain had stopped, and the wind was blowing away the clouds. Still, behind a distant green hill, the sky was dark and brooding. One could imagine an army of warriors waiting there, on black horses, ready to pound down into the valley. One could imagine anything in Ireland.

She reread the second line of the letter. "I look forward to seeing you next summer." She smiled and slipped it into the envelope.

She was homesick for the sounds of San Francisco Bay, the moaning foghorns, the impatient and angry toot of the tugs, the warning horns of the ferries. Sometimes she awoke suddenly at night, thinking she heard cable cars again. Or Mrs. Conner's voice in the hall, scolding a new maid. Or Joseph's slippered feet whispering on carpet.

It was so far away, almost unattainable. But between it and Ireland lay the possibility of Italy.

She took out another sheet of paper and the envelope that her aunt would mail for her after Kate had left.

Dear Kate,
You will get this after you've reached San Francisco.
There are things I wanted to say to you before you
leave Ireland, but I would not be able to tell the
truth if I have to look into your face.

I know what you have done for me, besides
saving my life more than once. Your eyes do not
keep secrets well, dear Kate. When we say good-
bye, both of us will know that we will not see each
other again, in any other place outside of Heaven.

You have taught me many things during our
time together. I learned to laugh harder than I
ever had before. I learned to accept my mother's
death. I learned to love a new land. I learned to
respect my talent. I learned what it means to have
a real friend.

Kate! Thank you!
Your loving sister,
Jolie

Kate left on Friday morning, with enough confusion to
make one think that the entire household was moving.
Jolie had gone downstairs earlier, cautiously, leaning
heavily on the arm of Aunt Elizabeth's maid, when no
one else was around to watch. It was important to her
that her aunt and Kate not concern themselves with her
at that time. It was difficult for her to breathe, but she
concentrated on hiding this.

Kate. She cared more for the hamper of linens
than she did for her own trunks, and she drove the
footmen to distraction with requests for more rope

tied tighter, and another label on this side and then on that side. Pocket, trying to interest Kate in the small bag she would be carrying herself, failed completely, and finally Jolie told the maid, "Hand it to her as you get in the carriage. She'll never listen to a word you're saying."

At the last moment, Jolie asked Pocket to bring down a certain package from under her bed. She handed it to Kate and saw that she truly had surprised her with half a dozen of the sort of silly romances they had read on their journey to Ireland.

"I've been hiding these since my trip to Dublin. You only thought I'd shown everything to you. There's another about the duchess and one about the illegitimate twins of the countess and her riding instructor—"

"Jolie!" Aunt Elizabeth cried as she came down the stairs to join them. "Surely you haven't given something like that to a young girl like Kate."

"Kate reads them by the dozen, Aunt," Jolie said, laughing.

Aunt Elizabeth rolled her eyes. "Well, I can't be held responsible for this. Now, Kate, are you sure you don't want us to pack another hamper of food for you?"

"We'll have more than enough to eat," Kate said. "Thank you for your generosity. Thank you for everything! I've never been happier than I've been here."

"You'll come back," Mrs. Cross said. "Everyone always comes back to Ireland."

Kate blinked back tears. "Yes, somehow I believe I will."

The moment had come. Kate's things had been

loaded on the carriage, and the footman and Pocket were waiting outside the door.

Kate went to Aunt Elizabeth first and said, "I shall remember you for the rest of my life."

Aunt Elizabeth cleared her throat. "And I shall remember you," she said.

Next, Kate went to Jolie and said, "I'm not saying good-bye to you. You have been a thorn in my flesh and a joy in my life. I'll envy you when you're in Italy, and I will see you when you're home again. And I promise you that I will overcharge you for bloomers when you come into the shop that I'll have one day."

Jolie smiled. "I'll pay any price, just to hear you laugh."

Kate was gone, her velvet skirt whispering as she hurried away. Aunt Elizabeth closed the door, sighed, and said, "It's as if a bright candle was put out, isn't it?"

"Yes. That describes a room when Kate leaves. Now will you call Mrs. Bridewell for me? I think I'll rest in my room until she comes."

"Oh, this has been too much for you!" her aunt cried. "You shouldn't have come downstairs."

"And why not?" Jolie said. "I felt more than well enough for that. But now I'm thirsty for some of the tea that Mrs. Bridewell brews for me. I never thought I'd admit it, but I've developed a taste for the stuff. Do you suppose she'll give me some to bring to Italy?"

Aunt Elizabeth, supporting Jolie as she climbed the stairs, said, "I believe she would give you anything you wanted. But what a strange woman she is. I trust her more than I trust any of the doctors. And I'm not the only one who feels this way. Did I tell you what happened to Mrs. McCoy when her last child was born . . ."

Jolie barely heard her. All her concentration was bent on putting one foot on the next step and then the other foot on the step above that. Her aunt helped her into bed and closed the curtains to shut out the gray day.

"I'll have Mrs. Bridewell here in a few minutes," she began.

But Mrs. Bridewell stepped through the door, pulling off her cape as she came. "I'm here," she said.

Aunt Elizabeth did not seem particularly surprised. "I'll see you before you go, Mrs. Bridewell," she said. "We'll have a little chat in the library. And I'll send hot water up here." As she left, she closed the door.

Mrs. Bridewell bent over Jolie. "Are you in pain?"

"Yes," Jolie gasped, free at last to confess it.

"I'll brew the tea," Mrs. Bridewell said. "Here, let me put another pillow behind you. I don't want you lying down now." She finally had Jolie sitting to her satisfaction, and then she began pulling packets and boxes from her bag. She always used a small teapot of her own, and a cup that only held a few teaspoons of tea. A maid came in silently with a pot of steaming water and set it on the table by the hearth. Mrs. Bridewell dribbled water into the teapot, drop by drop, whispering and humming.

Jolie watched, relaxing moment by moment. She knew this comforting routine, hidden from everyone in the household except her. After the tea, she would sleep for a while, and when she woke, she would be stronger, without pain for hours.

At last Mrs. Bridewell put the lid on the pot. She stood for a few moments, holding the pot in both hands while she bent her head over it, still humming. Then she poured the tea into the small cup and gave it to Jolie.

Jolie made a face, but she drank it down in three gulps. When she leaned back again, she smiled.

"I don't know if it's the tea or your humming, but I feel better already. I always do when you've come."

"My mother taught me to hum," Mrs. Bridewell said. She pulled a chair close to the bed, removed Jolie's glasses, and put them on the table. "It's not ordinary humming. There's a story in it, if you listen. Now pay attention and see if you can hear it. And when you've dropped off, I'll just run down and talk to your aunt for a while. But if you need me, I'll come right back up. We've all the time in the world."

Jolie closed her eyes and listened, and after a few moments, she thought she really did hear a story. She could almost *see* it. There was a ship sailing on a gentle sea, pushed by a warm wind toward a land where the air smelled of oranges and lemons, and the sun cast dark shadows under trees with shining green leaves. A cobbled street led up a hill, and Jolie walked along it, breathing easily, her legs strong again as they had been when she was a child. She carried a sketchbook under her arm, and she was wearing the green linen clothes Kate had made for her.

This must be Italy, she thought, wondering, *But is it?* She smiled and fell asleep.

"*Jolie? Oh, darling, were you sleeping? I'm so sorry.*"

"*Mother?*" Jolie sat up in bed, surprised.

Her mother, dressed in the beautiful gray Worth gown, her hair up, her diamond earrings glittering, put the cup of tea on Jolie's bedside table. "*I shouldn't have said anything. I didn't mean to wake you.*"

"*Well, now I'm wide awake, and I'm not a bit sorry,*" Jolie said. She reached for the tea. "*Tell me everything about the opera. Tell me what everyone said about your gown, and the earrings Father gave you. And don't leave out a single detail.*"

"*Of course I won't,*" her mother said. She settled herself on the edge of Jolie's bed. "*We have all the time in the world.*"

READ THE SEQUEL TO

A Sea So Far

RISING TIDE

It is 1908. Kate Keely has returned to a newly bustling San Francisco from her stay in Ireland—a trip she made as the hired companion to terminally ill Jolie Logan. Now, in the wake of Jolie's death, a grieving Kate needs to make a new life for herself.

She and her friend, Ellen Flannery, pool their hard-earned money and rent a small shop. There, they will sell handmade Irish linens and dresses to wealthy women and college students, or so they hope. But there are many obstacles for two untried girls trying to establish a business—and not all of them are professional. . . .

———◆———

Turn the page for a taste of *Rising Tide!*

Chapter 1

KATE

December 1908

"Kate, look at that!"

Katherine Keely looked up from her travel journal when Annie Prescott cried out, to catch a glimpse of a bonfire through the train window. But it was out of sight before she saw it clearly, and the train curved away along the track, moving south through the late evening toward California and home.

The sight of fire often made her uneasy, but Annie interrupted her worry by saying, "I saw dozens of children gathered around. It must be an early Christmas celebration. What fun!"

Kate's rigid spine relaxed. A celebration, not devastation. She had never completely recovered from the great San Francisco fire that had followed the earthquake more than two years before, and sometimes open flames triggered terrible memories. She never spoke of them, however. Few of the victims ever did.

"It's hard to think about Christmas when you're on a train," Kate said.

"We'll be home in time for it," Annie said. She smiled across the compartment at Kate and then went back to her book.

The train swayed just enough to cause Kate's pencil to add unexpected flourishes in her small leather journal, but she was accustomed to this. She and the Prescotts, her friends and traveling companions, had left New York four days earlier, and even though she had known the trip would be miserable in winter, she had not expected spending so many hours waiting for rails to be cleared of snow, or being sidetracked when a wealthy man's private train needed their engines to help it speed through a mountain pass, or encountering the beggars-turned-robbers who piled on the car ahead of hers at a meal stop, assaulting passengers and demanding money and jewelry before the men in the car overpowered them and threw them out. There was a great deal to put in a journal.

Kate, in the process of recording what she knew of the attempted robbery, paused long enough to look out the window again at the deepening twilight, and shook her head slowly. Perhaps the travel difficulties had been for the best after all. She had not had much time to worry about the uncertainty that was waiting for her in San Francisco or to brood about the tragedy she had left behind in Ireland.

The plans for independence that she had made while she was in Dublin might not work out now. She had been hired to care for Jolie Logan—and promised a reward for staying with the young invalid—but Jolie, who had become her close friend, had died in spite of everything. Now Kate was left in the kind of position she had always hated, unable to see a clear path ahead of her. How could she provide a living for her aunt and herself? Travel problems might even be looked at as a relief, since dealing with the delays, the noise, the smells, and the exasperation of being trapped in a car with mostly incompatible strangers offered an odd kind of diversion.

Kate's compartment door opened and Annie's husband, Peter, came in with news. "We'll be stopping in half an hour for dinner. Annie and I know this place very well, Kate. The food is good, and you must eat something this time. You've grown so thin that your aunt will think we broke our promise and didn't take care of you on the way home."

Kate closed the black leather journal, slipped it into her skirt pocket, and stood up stiffly. She had left Dublin for home in November and had spent nearly a week in cramped quarters aboard ship, then two weeks in a New York hotel waiting while Peter recovered from a particularly serious case of influenza, and then this train trip that seemed endless. Who wanted to eat? "I'll enjoy food more when I'm back in San Francisco," she said. She made a small effort to tidy her curly red hair, gave up, and asked Annie for help. "Aunt Grace always tells me that I look like a banshee."

Annie laughed, touched her own curly hair, and then took the brush that Kate handed her. "I hate my hair until I see someone struggling with curl papers or a crimping iron. There, now. You look fine. I'll get out my heavy coat—it's going to be cold at the station—and then perhaps I'll go visit with your new friends until we stop. What nice girls! We should all get together for dinner some time soon."

Kate, settling her small black hat in place, said, "I don't know how you do it. You must know people all over the world."

But Annie only laughed again. "We love to make new friends when we travel. And we'll travel for the rest of our lives, I hope."

Kate, almost eighteen, never wanted to leave California again. She had departed San Francisco in May, originally expecting to be home within six months, and was now barely able to hope that she would celebrate Christmas with her aunt. "You're braver than I," she said.

Annie paused, her coat slung over one arm. "No one is braver than you, Kate."

Kate looked down for a moment, long enough to be sure that her eyes would not fill with tears. "The hardest part is yet to come. I have to talk to Jolie's father about everything, and I dread it so much."

"He's had your cables and the telegrams you sent from New York," Peter protested. "And surely Jolie's aunt must have cabled him, too."

"But he'll want to know why I gave in to her demands and left her aunt's house when she was so ill," Kate said. She pulled her coat on over her jacket and picked up her gloves. "I guess we'd better get ready."

Kate and Annie had shared a compartment since they left New York, changing trains and enduring endless waits on platforms that all looked the same to Kate. Peter had always arranged to have a berth near their door, and during the day he often spent hours with them in the compartment. But Kate, restless and sick of travel, had changed places with him for several hours each morning, and so she had met two young women, Edith Jones and Adele Carson, who were moving from New York to San Francisco.

The passengers were stirring, gathering up heavy wraps. The air smelled of coal smoke coming from the inefficient heating stoves, kerosene lanterns, cigars, and travel-stained clothing. Kate looked forward to taking deep breaths as soon as she left the car. Cold, deep breaths. Perhaps she was hungry after all.

Edith and Adele smiled when they saw her. "Are you

feeling better now, Kate?" asked Edith, the bride-to-be who had been willing to cross a continent to marry an old friend who was doing well in the business of rebuilding San Francisco.

Kate assured Edith that she had had a chance to rest, although that had not been strictly the case. Adele got up and pulled her heavy cape off the back of her red velvet seat, settling it around her shoulders. She was younger than Edith, closer to Kate's age, and she was planning to live with her grandparents in San Francisco. "They're awfully stuffy, but anything is better than working in a New York shirtwaist factory," she had told Kate.

The train stopped at a small station platform, where the frozen slush was stained black from coal dust, and two dozen beggars wrapped in blankets and rags watched sullenly. There was a delay before the passengers were let off, and the porter told them that someone had been injured in the robbery and now was being taken off the train for belated medical treatment. At last they were set free. The passengers hurried to find dinner, most turning their faces away from the outstretched dirty hands. The beggars at the first stations on the journey west had evoked pity. By now the travelers were leery of them, especially after the attack on the people in the other car.

Peter steered his wife, Kate, and her new friends toward a restaurant he knew very well, and they settled themselves at a long table where Peter ordered for them all. The meal was served promptly, which was a good thing because they had only forty-five minutes to eat and return to the train. Kate was hungry after all, and she ate fried pork chops and stewed tomatoes with more enthusiasm than she could have imagined earlier.

"Two days to Christmas," Adele said, as she folded her napkin and put it beside her empty plate. "I promised my grandparents that I'd be there in time to celebrate with them. But I heard the conductor say that there had been snow slides ahead of us."

Peter shook his head. "Don't say something like that aloud. I'm determined that we'll be home tomorrow, right on schedule."

"That still leaves enough time for the train to be derailed," Adele said, and everyone laughed, although Kate had to force herself to join in. She knew she might enjoy talking about this trip one day, but not yet. Not yet.

They stumbled back to the train platform over frozen ruts of mud and snow. The beggars were still on the platform, deliberately jostling passengers as they attempted to board. A woman wrapped in a filthy shawl grabbed at Kate's sleeve, but Peter intervened, ordering the woman to let go. Kate rushed up the steps and inside the car.

"Here, Kate!" Peter called out, close behind her. "Isn't this yours?" He held out the small leather travel journal.

"Did that woman have it?" Kate asked, surprised. She had made the skirt she was wearing, and the pockets were deep and concealed in the side seams to protect her from pickpockets.

"No, it was lying on the snow," Peter said. "Unless she had it and then dropped it."

The passengers crowded before and behind Kate, and she was moved along through the car, unable to examine the journal until she reached her compartment. And then she saw, astonished, that it was not hers.

Peter shut the compartment door behind Kate and Annie and threw off his coat. "I'll sit with you ladies for a while," he said. "What's wrong, Kate?"

Kate held up the opened journal. "This isn't mine," she said. She showed it to Peter and Annie. "See? It's just like it, though."

"Is there a name inside?" Annie asked, looking over Kate's shoulder.

Kate examined the first pages. "No, no name. Not even initials." She handed the journal back to Peter and said, "You'd better ask the people in the car. I know I'd hate to lose my journal. Somebody's probably missing it already."

Peter left again, and while he was gone, the porter came to make up the two beds in the compartment. Peter returned, still holding the small black book. "No one claimed it," he said. "It's possible that it belongs to someone in another car, but the porters are making up the berths now, so I'll find the owner tomorrow. Can I do anything for either of you?"

"We're fine," Annie told him. "One more night in the train, and after that we'll have beds that don't sway. But I'm not sure I'll be able to sleep then."

Kate, thinking of the small room she would share with her aunt in the Flannery boardinghouse, smiled to herself. She would be grateful for it, after being confined in even smaller places for so long. Best of all was the chance that she and her aunt might find an apartment she could afford in bustling, extravagant San Francisco and have their own home. It would be possible—if Jolie Logan's father still intended to give her the money he had promised when she had agreed to go to Ireland with his daughter.

Kate had never told anyone about the promise, thank goodness, because now she was not sure she had earned it. Dr. Logan's intention was that Jolie would be launched as a full-time traveler, like the Prescotts. But he had not faced the truth about her health.

Kate, trying to shake creases out of her hopelessly wrinkled travel suit, sighed. Whether she got the money or not, she would have to find a way to earn enough to support her aunt and herself. Aunt Grace had encouraged her and Ellen Flannery to open a small shop and be independent—and Kate and Ellen were saving money toward that goal—but San Francisco was expensive, and never more so than now, while it was rebuilding. The small combined savings of the girls might not be enough to rent a shop, even for a short while. Kate desperately needed Dr. Logan's help.

But his chronically ill daughter had died within hours of Kate's leaving her, and who knew whether or not he would hold her responsible?

"What was the big sigh for?" Annie asked as she brushed her hair.

Kate shivered and crawled into her narrow bed. "I'm just tired, I guess," she said. "And homesick. I'm close enough to San Francisco now to admit it."

They had breakfast the next morning in a hotel dining room near the station, eating quickly because the service had been slow and reluctant. Peter had asked as many passengers as he could find about the journal, but no one claimed it.

"It's yours now, Kate," he said, pushing it across the table to her.

"I don't feel right about taking it," she said slowly. "You're the one who found it."

"I read a few pages last night," Peter confessed. "You're the right one to take charge of it. Only you, Kate."

"Why?" Kate asked, surprised. She opened the journal and looked down at the unfamiliar, angular handwriting.

"Because the writer is also a reluctant traveler, Kate," Peter said. "You'll find a soul mate on the pages."

Kate made a small face. "Soul mate," she said. "How do you know the writer is a man?"

"Women don't usually complain about the quality of their cigars," Peter said, and he and Annie laughed.

Back on the train, she traded seats with Peter and opened the stranger's journal. She felt as if she was prying—and of course she was—so she read the first entry with a flushed face.

Boston. I visited my brother's grave on the day I arrived. The leaves on the nearby trees were burning red and yellow against a lonely gray sky, and after a while a bitter wind tore some of them loose. Boston is so far away from home, and the ocean is all wrong, supporting sunrise instead of sunset. Jeffrey commented on that in a letter once, saying that it depressed him. I wondered if he thought of it at the end.

His lawyer was with me, and we went to the stonecutter's to arrange for a headstone, which will not be set in place until after I have left. I feel guilty for not staying, but October is nearly over, and I want to be home before travel becomes even more difficult.

My brother's affairs took a week to conclude, and on the last day the lawyer offered me a cigar, which I accepted, although I suspected that it would be vile. It was. But then, I am not a smoker. Jeffrey was. My brother was many things that I am not.

But his life has been finished, as if he were a book

someone read and put aside. Now I am all that is left of
the family. I had sworn to myself that I would not seek
out Isabel, but I went to her uncle's house against my
better judgment, where I learned that she had left imme-
diately after Jeffrey died and returned to her parents.

I packed up those things of Jeffrey's that I wanted to
keep and arranged to have them shipped home. He had
a small blank leather journal that I decided to use myself
on the journey back. Who knows—perhaps I shall have a
profound thought or two. Or perhaps, with luck, the trip
will be too boring to record.

I am far from home and homesick.

Kate shut the journal abruptly and tucked it into her
pocket, next to her own journal. How sad, she thought.
Another person counting the days.

Kate got off the train in Oakland late on the day before
Christmas. Her aunt was waiting for her, crying and reaching out for a hug. The entire Flannery family was there,
too, with Ellen laughing as she hugged Kate, and Hugh,
red-faced and wearing a stiff new suit, clasping her hand so
hard that she winced. Mrs. Flannery and young Joe pushed
close to Kate to welcome her home, and Mrs. Flannery
added, "I won't believe you're here until we're on the ferry."

"I won't believe it until I unpack," Kate said.

She wondered where the journal writer was that night,

as she crossed San Francisco Bay toward the city where she had been born. Was he home at last, or had he another journey waiting for him before he saw familiar faces again? She would read his journal—probably—but not for a while. She did not even want to look through her own. Half smiling, she wondered if she had finally reached a place in her life when she would be glad to be bored.

In the last moments on the ferry, she waved at Adele and Edith, caught in the crowd and too far away to introduce to her friends, and then her eyes turned to the city lights. Home.

She was so tired that she was barely aware of the trip in the automobile Hugh had borrowed from friends for the occasion. Ellen had chattered constantly the whole way out Market Street from the ferry dock, in spite of her mother's admonitions to hush, and Aunt Grace never let loose of Kate's hand. Young Joe Flannery, sitting in front between his mother and Hugh, gawked over the back of the seat and grinned, showing big teeth, every time Kate spoke.

Here they were. The big, shabby boardinghouse had never seemed more inviting. Hugh helped Kate from the automobile and she looked up—to see a new face watching from the window over the porch.

"Is that a new boarder?" Kate said as she started up the porch steps beside Mrs. Flannery and her aunt, while the Flannery children carried her suitcases.

"Oh, that's just Thalia Rutledge," Aunt Grace said. "I

wrote you about the family. Here, dear, hurry inside where it's warm."

"What kind of name is Thalia?" Mrs. Flannery muttered. "It's foolish. And so are her parents. What was wrong with just plain old 'Polly'?"

"Oh, Ma, what do you care?" Ellen protested irritably. "She can't help what her parents call her. They're actors! Let the kid alone."

Home, Kate thought. And nothing had changed. She smiled.

But Thalia Rutledge, watching from a darkened landing on the stairs, was not smiling.